The 9ᵗʰ man

the 9th man

gay mystery by

Dorien Grey

**e-Book Division
GLB Publishers**

San Francisco

Published in the United States by
GLB Publishers
P.O. Box 78212, San Francisco, CA 94107 USA

Cover by GLB Publishers

ISBN 1-879194-78-3

Library of Congress Card Number:

00-110115

Number Two in the Dick Hardesty Series

2001

In memory

of Ray

with love

CHAPTER 1

It's hard to remember, now, that there was a time not so long ago when all it took to do whatever you wanted was to find someone willing to do it with you—when the highest "wages of sin" you might have to pay was a case of clap. It was a different time, and a different world, and I miss it.

* * *

It was hotter than hell, the air conditioner hadn't worked since the Titanic went down, and I was in no mood for the bleached-blond queen who came swishing across the room toward me after making an entrance that made me wonder whatever happened to Loretta Young. There were times when I almost wished I had a few straight clients, and this was one of those times. Still, I told myself, it isn't the principle of the thing, it's the money.

I stood up and extended my hand. As I expected, the proffered appendage was limp and vaguely clammy.

"Mr. Rholfing." I made it a statement, not a question. Clients, I've found, expect you to be decisive. Authoritative. Butch. It's bullshit, but it works.

"Yes, Mr. Hardesty." Jesus, he sounded as nelly as he looked. "I'm *so* glad you could see me." I felt his eyes giving my entire body a radar scan.

He was wearing one of those cloying perfumes/colognes that emanate an almost visible fog around the wearer.

"Have a chair," I said, indicating the one that would have been upwind if there'd been any movement of air through the open window, which there wasn't.

I sat down behind my desk and watched as Rholfing fluttered down, with considerable butt-wiggling, and immediately crossed his legs at the knee. He was dressed all in perma-starched white, with a flaming yellow ascot which missed his hair color by about eight shades. He looked like a butter-pecan ice cream cone with delusions of grandeur. After the talcum had settled, I sat back in my own chair and forced myself to stare directly at my prospective client—mentally picturing a maraschino cherry and some chopped nuts atop the carefully coifed curls.

Rholfing leaned forward, crossing his wrists on his crossed knees, and said simply: "Someone has killed my lover."

Why me, Lord? Why do I get all the cracked marbles?

We stared at one another in silence for a moment or two until I finally managed to remind myself that that's what I'm in business for: to solve other people's mysteries.

"Any idea who?" I asked.

"How should *I* know?" he said, exasperated, his manicured hands fluttering up a short distance from his knees, only to settle back, studiedly.

"Well, at the risk of sounding a bit like a B movie," I said, "isn't this a matter for the police?"

Rholfing stared at me as though I'd just farted in church.

"The *police* all but said that he committed suicide. The *police*," he said finally, "eat shit. Somebody killed him."

The thought flashed through my mind that anyone sharing an evening, let alone a life, with the character in front of me might well be a candidate for suicide. "Exactly what makes you think he was murdered?" I asked, choosing not to get into a long discussion of the merits and flaws of law enforcement.

"Bobby was 27 years old, healthy as a horse—hung like one, too—and never had a sick day in his life, unless you count hangovers. Personally, I don't. And all of a sudden he's dead in some cheap, tacky hotel room without a mark on him and the *police* think it was suicide!"

"I assume there was an autopsy," I said. "What did they say about that?"

"Oh, they said several things, none of which a lady cares to repeat. The gist of it was that while it was perfectly all right for a fruit like me to come down to the morgue to identify the body, since I was neither a blood relative nor his legal guardian, I had no right whatsoever to any information other than that he's dead—which any fool could see, with him lying there on that fucking slab!"

"And that was it?"

Rholfing took a small white handkerchief from his shoulder bag and dabbed at the corners of his mouth. He then carefully folded it, returned it to the bag, zipped the bag shut, and re-creased the already razor-sharp crease in his trousers with thumb and forefinger before finally re-meeting my gaze.

"Not quite," he said. "Two of the burly cretins took me into a small room and subtly asked me what my experience had been with poisons. *Poisons*! *Me*! I was tempted to tell them to drop by some afternoon for tea and I'd see what I could do, but I'd just had the fumigators in. *Me*! Lucretia Borgia! Can you imagine?"

As a matter of fact, I could.

"Now, I may be a fairy," he continued, smoothing down the back of his hair with one hand, "but I certainly am not stupid! Their refusing to tell me how he died in one breath and asking me about poisons in the next was about as subtle as a lighted match on the Hindenburg.

"Bobby was murdered. There's no question about it. And knowing how the *police* in this city feel about faggots, the only way anyone is going to find out who killed Bobby is for *me* to hire *you*. You come…" (he gave me a smile I'm sure he meant to be disarming, but came across outright lecherous) "…very highly recommended."

"Thanks," I said, awkwardly. I never did learn how to accept compliments very well—even those without hooks in them. "Have you spoken to Bobby's parents about this?" I asked.

"What parents?" Rholfing asked, haughtily. "He told me he had a grandfather back in Utah somewhere, but he never mentioned parents, if he ever had any."

"So can you tell me anything about Bobby that might help?" I asked.

"Well, he was a tramp—that much I know. He'd go home with anything in pants. I told him I was going to get him his own portable glory hole and put it out in the street in front of the apartment. At least that way I'd know where he was all the time."

"Did the police say anything about drugs?"

Rholfing thought a moment, lips pursed, nose wrinkled, brows knit, eyes looking upward at nothing. "I don't think so. Just poisons."

"Did he use drugs?" I asked.

Rholfing sighed. "No, thank God. That was one of his good points—about his only one, come to think of it: he never got mixed up with drugs. Oh, he'd smoke a joint now and then, but I guess we *all* do, don't we?" He gave me a conspiratorial wink—the kind you can see from the top row of the balcony—and that coy/lecherous smile again.

I didn't say anything for a moment (that's a bad habit I have; when I don't have anything to say, I tend not to say anything—bugs the shit out of a lot of people), and Rholfing sat there looking more and more uncomfortable as the seconds dragged on. He pulled a monogrammed handkerchief from God knows where and began waving it gently back and forth beneath his chin. A tiny droplet of perspiration crept from his hairline and meandered its way across his left temple.

Finally, he couldn't stand it. "Well? Will you take the case?"

"Okay," I said. "But I don't have much to go on." God! Where had I heard that line before?

"Well, *find* something," Rholfing blurted, revealing the rolled-steel interior behind that whipped-cream and lace facade. "*You're* the big, strong detective. To the cops he's just another dead fag, and good riddance—but nobody kills my lover and gets away with it." He must have anticipated my next comment, because he hastened to add: "Don't worry about the money. Daddy has five or six acres of downtown Fort Worth, and he'll give me anything I want just for me to stay the hell away from there."

I found myself in something of a quandary. I had—clichés aside—very little to go on. Given Rholfing's account of the circumstances of the death, however accurate or inaccurate they may have been, and despite his denial of his lover's drug use, the obvious assumption was that it was very likely a routine drug overdose. But that's why people hire me in the first place;

if they knew all the answers, who'd need a detective? The police were notoriously uncooperative in anything that smacked of homosexuality. And I wasn't exactly in a position to pass up a potential client—particularly one whose Daddy had five or six acres of downtown Fort Worth.

I thought of Tim Jackson, a sometime-trick and pretty good friend of mine who works in the county coroner's office. I'd never had the occasion to use his professional services, but maybe now was the time.

"Okay, Mr. Rholfing; I'll check it out," I said. "But don't expect miracles." I thought he was going to leap across the desk and kiss me. Fortunately, he didn't.

"Now, about my fee…" I began, but he cut me off by digging into his shoulder bag and coming up with a bunch of crisp, new $100 bills.

"Will this be enough? For a retinue, or whatever in hell it is you call it?"

"Retainer, and it'll do just fine," I said, making a conscious effort not to grab it out of his hand.

"You *will* call me, won't you?" he said, rising out of his chair as graceful as a hot-air balloon and again giving me the radar scan. "Even if you don't have anything to report, I'd appreciate your keeping in… *close*…touch." He used one hand to adjust his shoulder bag while the other made an inspection of the back of his shirt, pulling and tugging at imaginary wrinkles. "Perhaps you could stop by for a drink some evening?" He sounded like Delilah asking Samson to stop by for a haircut. "You *do* have my name and address, don't you?"

I assured him I had written them down when he called for the appointment, resisting the temptation to speculate that every tearoom wall in town had his number. I rose and he, eyes glued to my crotch, offered me a dead hand at the end of a limp wrist. I wasn't sure whether I was supposed to kiss it or shake it, so I took the latter course, and he turned on his little ballerina feet and swished to the door.

"Oh, there is one little thing," I called after him as his hand reached for the knob. He turned quickly, eyes sparkling coquettishly.

"Yes?"

"About your lover."

"Who?"

"Your lover. Bobby."

"Oh. Yes." He looked disappointed.

"It might help if I knew his last name."

"McDermott," he said over his shoulder as he opened the door. "Bobby McDermott." And with that, he was gone.

I sat back down, leaned back in my chair, and put my thumbnail between my teeth—a dumb habit, I'll admit, but that's the kind of thing you do when you go from three packs of cigarettes a day to nothing. I stared at the door for a minute, then pulled my thumb out of my mouth, reached for a note pad, and wrote "Bobby McDermott."

Part of me felt slightly guilty for taking Rholfing's money; one call to Tim Jackson should confirm that it was drugs and give me whatever other information I might need to wrap the whole matter up.

It was five thirty; too late to reach Tim at the office but, if I waited a few minutes, I could probably reach him at home. Suddenly, I was looking at my crotch, and it was reminding me of how long it had been since I'd seen Tim.

It was too hot to wait in the office, so I decided to go down the street to Hughie's and have a drink. I could call Tim from there. Thin wisps of Rholfing's cologne still hung in the air so, cursing the broken air conditioner and hoping it wouldn't rain, I left the window wide open as I closed the door behind me.

*   *   *

Hughie's is a hustler bar about two blocks from the office. I like to stop in every now and then to watch the hustlers and johns go through their little mating dances; the hustlers preening and strutting, or just standing around trying to out-butch one another; the johns— middle class business executives, most of them—sidling up, pretending they've just wandered into the bar by accident. The "casual" opening remarks ("Sure is hot today, isn't it?" "Say, that's a nice-looking shirt you've got on." "Can I buy you a drink?"). The john buying the hustler a drink, then two; the exit with the john looking nervous but trying to act cool, the hustler sauntering casually through the door as if he were just stepping outside to see if it's raining.

The whole place has a sort of morbid fascination, if you like living vicariously, which I don't. I go there mainly because it's close and because you can often learn things at Hughie's you couldn't learn elsewhere without a lot of hassle.

Out of curiosity, when I ordered my beer I asked Bud, the bartender, if he'd ever heard of a guy called Bobby McDermott.

"Sorry, Dick," he said, drawing a dark into a frosty glass (that's another reason I go to Hughie's—it's a dive, but they frost their beer glasses, and it's one of the few places that has dark beer on tap). "Nobody's much on names around here, in case you hadn't noticed. What's the dude look like?"

I had another slight pang of guilt when I realized I had no idea.

"I dunno," I said, trying to sound casual. "It's not important; just thought you might know him."

"Huh-uh," Bud said, taking my money. "I don't think so. But if anybody'd know him, it'd be Tessie." He looked around. "Not here right now. If he's not here for happy hour, he'll be in around ten or eleven."

"Thanks, Bud," I called to his back as he moved off down the bar to serve another customer. I took a couple deep draughts, fought back a belch, and rummaged through my change for a coin. I waited until there was a lull on the jukebox and went to the phone to dial Tim.

It rang four times and I was just about to hang up when Tim answered.

"'Lo?" Jesus, even his voice was sexy. I kicked myself for not having kept in closer touch with him.

"Hi, Tim," I said, hoping he wouldn't remember just how long it had been. "It's Dick. Hardesty. Just get home?"

"A while ago. I was just getting ready to hop into the shower.

Care to join me?"

"Only if you'll agree to drop the soap," I said.

Tim laughed. "They don't call me 'Old Slippery Fingers' for nothing. Where the hell have you been anyway? I thought you'd given me up for lost."

"No way. It's just that I've been…ah…you know…" Always quick with an answer, that's me.

"That's okay," Tim said, laughing again. "I know how it is. So when are we going to get together?"

"Well, as a matter of fact, there was something I wanted to talk over with you. You going to be home for awhile?"

"Sure; I'm in for the night. Come on over—it'll be nice to see you again. We can talk over old times and…uh…see what comes up."

"Still World's Champion Prickteaser, I see," I said. "See you in ten minutes." I hung up, went back to the bar to chug-a-lug the rest of my beer, waved goodbye to Bud, and sauntered out the door like a hustler checking to see if it was raining.

*   *   *

Tim's apartment is a ten-minute walk from Hughie's. I made it in seven. I rang the bell, and the door opened the length of the safety- latch chain. Tim's curly brown hair appeared first as he peered around the corner of the door, then his bright blue eyes and big, shit-eating grin.

"Hi," he said in a sotto-voiced stage whisper and looking me over with mock seriousness. "What's the password?"

"Necrophilia," I whispered, and Tim leaned against the door, laughing, and closed it. I could hear the chain being released. Then the door opened again, wider this time, and Tim's head and bare shoulders appeared from behind it.

"Come on in," he laughed. He apparently had just gotten out of the shower and was wearing nothing but a towel and an ear-to-ear grin. He closed the door behind me and refastened the chain.

"There's a drag queen two doors down who's always coming

by for a cup of Vaseline or something every time he knows I'm home," Tim said, still smiling. "Actually, he's just hot for m'bod."

"Well, he'll just have to take a number and stand in line like everybody else," I said, grabbing him in a bear hug and lifting him off the floor. Tim threw his arms around my neck and returned the hug—then his eyes grew wide and he got that little-boy look that always made me melt.

"To paraphrase my good friend Mae West," he said, staring directly into my eyes with the tip of his nose pressed against mine, "is that a gun in your pocket, or are you just glad to see me?"

"Damn," I said, still holding him off the floor, "and I wanted it to be a surprise." I opened my mouth wide and, with a loud hiss, clamped my lips wetly on the base of his neck at the shoulder, applying a slow pressure with my teeth.

Tim struggled to get away. "You give me a hickey, you bastard, and your ass is grass."

I set him down and held him at arm's length, noticing with pleasure that I'd found his "On" button.

"You want to talk now, or later?" he asked.

"Later," I said, unfastening his towel and letting it drop to the floor. Tim might have the face and body of a teenager, but he packed an adult's equipment—and then some.

We made our way to the bedroom and Tim sprawled on the bed on his stomach, facing me and watching me as I stood just inside the door and undressed. It was all part of the ritual we followed on those occasions—too rare, I realized as I watched him watching me; when we got together; neither of us wasted much time in idle chit-chat. As I took off my pants and shorts, Tim's face slowly broke into that wicked-little-kid grin and, when I stood there fully naked, he slowly crooked his index finger at me. As I walked over to the bed, straight toward him, Tim opened his mouth and slowly extended his tongue. Bull's-eye!

*   *   *

"Cigarette?" he asked, leaning across me for an ashtray on the night stand.

"Gave 'em up," I said, smugly.

"You? Liggett & Myers' best friend?" He paused to light up. "I'm proud of you. Really. It's a filthy habit." And he blew a long stream of smoke into my face.

"You little…" I said, lunging out to tickle him under the arm, which always drove him up the wall. He shrieked and rolled away from me, almost falling off the bed in the process.

"Don't! Please! I'll be good! Honest!" he gasped between arias of laughter and frantic flailing trying to fend off my insistent tickling. Finally, fearful that the neighbors might be considering calling the police, I stopped.

Tim lay limp, catching his breath. He took a long drag from his cigarette, which had somehow come through the struggle unscathed, and carefully blew the smoke away from me. After a minute, he plumped up his pillow and scooted himself up on the bed, his back against the headboard.

"Okay, so let's talk," he said.

"About what?" I asked.

"About whatever it was you called me about," he said with a grin.

I duplicated his pillow-plumping and hoisted myself up beside him. "You know I hate to mix business with pleasure, but…"

"Yeah, yeah, I know. So 'but' what?"

"Your office had a case recently—you probably don't remember it with all those stiffs you have coming and going. Mostly going. But this one was kind of different. Young guy named Bobby McDermott; 27."

Tim muttered something under his breath—it sounded like "Fuck!"—and stared into the ashtray balanced on his stomach.

"What?" I asked.

Tim turned his head and looked at me, strangely, his eyes searching my face. He said nothing.

I felt a twinge of guilt. "Hey, Tim, I'm sorry," I said. "I know I don't have any right to butt into your business…"

Tim shrugged and relaxed a little. "It's okay," he said, finally. "Yeah, I remember Bobby McDermott. What about him?"

"The police apparently indicated to his lover that he killed himself. Probably poison. His lover swears he was murdered."

Tim stubbed his cigarette into the ashtray, staring at it and continuing to tamp it long after it was out. "What makes him think that?"

Patience was never one of my greater virtues, and obviously Tim knew something he wasn't too eager to share with me.

"Come on, Tim! The guy's 27. Healthy as a horse—hung like one, too, I understand. No apparent problems—unless you count the lover, but that's another story. Apparently the only thing he was addicted to is sex, and I've never heard of anyone fucking themselves to death, have you?" Tim shrugged, avoiding my eyes. "And then the cops ask the lover what he knows about poisons. That strikes me as more than a little strange; they don't ask about drugs, but poisons."

Tim pursed his lips, thought a moment, then turned to me with a deep sigh. "Well," he said, shaking his head, "somebody was bound to catch on, sooner or later."

"Catch on to what?" I asked, with a strange feeling in the pit of my stomach.

"First of all, he didn't die of drugs; it was poison. Cyanide, to be exact. Apparently inhaled. Secondly, I'm pretty sure it wasn't suicide."

"What makes you think that?" I asked.

"Apart from the fact that cyanide is a pretty esoteric way for anybody to commit suicide, how would someone like McDermott manage to get hold of it? It's not impossible to come by, but it's not exactly a household product. But what really blows a hole in the suicide theory—and a little detail that the cops apparently chose to overlook—is that from what I understand, there was absolutely nothing in the room to indicate how he managed to inhale cyanide. No bottles, vials, inhalers, rags, nothing."

"Weird," I said, the butterflies still there.

"It gets weirder when you consider that Bobby McDermott wasn't the first case we've had like it in the past couple weeks. He's the sixth one."

CHAPTER 2

It took a second to sink in. Suddenly, I wanted a cigarette more than anything in the world.

"What do you mean, he's the sixth one?" I asked, trying to sound as casual as possible.

Tim flopped over on his stomach and bunched his pillow under his chest, supporting himself on his elbows and looking at me direct and hard. I could almost see his mind working, sending flashes of thought through his eyes.

"Look, Dick, I like you, and I think you're the kind of guy who can be trusted. But to be honest we don't really know each other all that well, and I could lose my job and possibly get my ass busted over this thing. I just don't know if it's worth it."

I reached out and put my hand on his shoulder. "Hey, I understand, Tim. But six people? Something's going on, and I think six people's lives are worth a hell of a lot."

"Well, there's this, too: it's not just six people; it's six guys, and from what I know, six gay guys," Tim said. "And of course you're right. But they've managed to keep the whole thing quiet so far—either the media hasn't caught wind of it yet, or they're being asked to keep a lid on it to prevent another Freeway Strangler or Trashbag Murders circus."

"How long a period did you say we're we talking about?" I asked.

"Two months."

"And how do you know they were all gay?"

"Six single men in their late 20s on up? Only one of them was identified by a blood relative—a father who made the identification but refused to accept the body because he said his son had died years ago. Two of them had admitted lovers—one, McDermott's, an obvious fag, the other a guy I'd talked to in the bars—three were identified by 'roommates' I'll bet my bottom dollar are 'our people', and one by a friend who went into hysterics and said a lot of things he shouldn't have."

"And all of them were killed by cyanide?"

Tim nodded. "Cyanide, prussic acid, the same thing. All

inhaled, with an extremely high concentration of residue in one nostril, and in a circle the size of a dime on one thumb. Give you any clue?"

"Poppers?" I said. "They thought they were taking a hit of amyl nitrate and it was cyanide instead? Jesus!" Just about every gay I knew used amyl for a quick high; especially on the dance floor and during sex. One sniff and the top of your head sort of goes off. Cyanide in an amyl bottle or an inhaler!

"Yep," Tim said. "One deep whiff, and it's all over! About one minute, maximum. And considering the victim is inhaling deeply through just one nostril, it doesn't take much; just 300 parts of hydrogen cyanide per million parts of air, and you're gone."

"And what are the police doing about all this?" I asked.

Before answering, Tim reached across me to pick up a pack of cigarettes and an ashtray from the night stand.

"Not much, I'm afraid," he said, rolling over onto his back and putting the ashtray on his chest. "Their first theory apparently was that somebody'd poisoned a batch of poppers, and that whoever was unlucky enough to get a contaminated bottle ended up randomly dead. In case you hadn't noticed they've yanked all the amyl out of the gay baths, bookstores and head shops—they haven't found anything, of course, but I don't think they care much; it just gives them another excuse to harass gay businesses."

"Just performing a public service," I said, managing a weak grin.

Tim snorted. "The poisoned-batch-and-random-death theory wasn't valid from the beginning, anyway."

"Because...?" I prompted.

"First, because amyl's sort of a social thing—not many guys use it when they're alone. Secondly, because since no amyl bottles were found at any of the scenes, somebody had to have taken them. And can you imagine any random group of guys watching their partners take a hit of amyl, drop dead, and then having the presence of mind to just pick up the bottle and leave without saying anything to anyone?"

"Nope," I said.

"Nope," he repeated.

We laid there in silence for a moment while my mind sifted through everything Tim had said.

Finally, Tim tamped his cigarette out in the ashtray on his chest and reached past me again to return the ashtray to the night stand.

"You know," he continued as though he'd never stopped talking, "the ironic thing about the cyanide-laced amyl theory is that amyl nitrate is actually an antidote for cyanide. A lot of cyanide in a little amyl might kill somebody, but probably not instantly; and from all evidence we have, these six guys went immediately. So I'd say somebody—one person— emptied and cleaned an amyl bottle and filled it with a pure hydrogen cyanide. Probably used sulfuric acid as the activating agent."

I thought a minute, then theorized: "So we're looking for a chemist."

He stuck out his tongue just far enough to pick a small piece of tobacco from it, and shook his head. "Not necessarily. All somebody would really need is a basic knowledge of chemistry, a little cyanide, and some sulfuric acid."

"Oh, yeah," I said. "A little cyanide; aisle 4 at your local supermarket."

"You'd be surprised how common cyanide is," Tim said. "It's got a lot industrial applications. It can be toxic, but not necessarily lethal when handled properly.

"As for what else the police might be doing, they're not exactly sharing much information. We've done our best to convince them that it's unlikely anyone is poisoning batches of amyl nitrate, so I think they're slowly swinging to the 'serial killer' scenario. They'll probably like that one once they settle on it; it's a lot easier than trying to find out what all these guys have in common."

"Maybe they don't," I said. "Maybe it is a serial killer— though I've got a gut feeling it isn't." I shook my head. "I still can't understand why, no matter how it happened, nobody outside your office and the cops know about it?" I asked.

"Lots of reasons, I suppose," Tim said. "'Ongoing investigation.' 'Avoid panic.' You name it. Now, of course, if you had six dead heterosexuals all killed by something as exotic as cyanide and all in the space of two months, they'd be calling out the guard. Families screaming bloody murder —no pun intended—, the police out to polish up the department's image; it's all over the news. But six gay men in a city this size—six gays who apparently have nothing whatever in common except being gay and dead…" He paused and shook his head slowly. "They don't look alike, they aren't all the same age, they don't all work together, and as far as we can tell, don't even know the same people. For all intents and purposes, these are just six isolated, unrelated deaths."

"But the death certificates have to list the cause of death," I said. "Surely some of the families must have made inquiries."

"Sure they did. As individual families from all over the country making individual inquiries about individual deaths in which the death certificate shows the cause of death to be 'respiratory arrest.' That could mean almost anything. Plus, they haven't the foggiest idea that there have been similar deaths. They're assured the police are 'investigating,' and if that doesn't satisfy them, they're given not-so-subtle reference to how unstable and prone to suicide and random violence faggots are 'known' to be. And what's a family who lives in Sheep-dip, Montana going to do about it except grieve? Not much, I can tell you."

"And the gays—the lovers and friends who don't know there have been other victims—don't want to make waves," I finished Tim's reasoning. Tim nodded. "Except one," I added.

"The word's gone around to the privileged few in the office who know about the whole thing that the first person to start making waves about this will be very sorry, indeed. And since it isn't exactly the world's best kept secret that I'm gay, everybody has their beady little eyes cocked in my direction." Tim sighed. "And so now you know and I'm going to have to trust you not to get me in trouble. Pregnant, maybe, but not in trouble."

I pulled him to me and gave him a long hug. "Trust me, kid," I said, feeling—and, I'm afraid, sounding—very much like Humphrey Bogart.

A low, rumbling growl made Tim jump. "Supper time," he said, grinning sheepishly and patting his stomach. "Can you stay for dinner? I've got some home-made lasagna in the freezer."

"How can I resist?" I said. "I'm free for the night. Or at least reasonable."

"You're welcome to stay over," he said, making a little let-your-fingers-do-the-walking movement over my chest, letting his index finger trip over my right nipple, his hand falling into the space between my arm and chest.

"Invitation gratefully accepted," I said, drawing him closer. But my romantic intentions were interrupted by another bed-shaking stomach rumble—from me, this time.

"Saved by the bell," Tim laughed, moving quickly out of my arms and off the bed. "Let's eat."

*   *   *

The next morning, over coffee, I asked Tim if he would do me one more favor. He gave me his wide-eyed-shock look.

"Don't you Scorpio's ever get enough?"

I grinned. "As a matter of fact, no. But that wasn't what I was talking about."

"The deaths," he said.

"Afraid so. As long as I'm being paid to find out who killed Bobby McDermott, I don't have much choice but to follow every mud-rut path until I find the highway. Could you get me whatever you can on the other five guys? Next of kin, lovers, addresses… anything that might help?"

"You're going to tackle the whole thing on your own?"

"God, I hope not," I said. "But I think we both agree that there's probably just one guy out there responsible for all six deaths; and as I said last night, whether or not he's targeting specific people or if he's just picking up tricks at random is something somebody has to find out. Will you help?"

Tim got up from the table to pour himself another cup of coffee. He returned to the table and sat down again before answering. "Why not? So I lose my job? So I get a lifetime supply of parking tickets? So the cops see to it that I'm shot while resisting arrest for jaywalking? Sure, I'll help you. But just remember that everybody's watching me like a hawk. I don't know how much information I can get to you."

"Anything will help. And I'll owe you."

Tim's eyes took on a devilish glint. "I'll remember that," he said.

*   *   *

"Why, of course I have a picture of Bobby." The voice was as irritatingly nelly over the phone as it was in person.

"That's fine, Mr. Rholfing," I said, before he had a chance to say anything else. "Why don't I drop by in about an hour to pick it up?"

There was a pause, during which I swore I could hear the wheels spinning around in his marcelled little head.

"Why, of course," he said, finally, in a voice so coy I could almost see his eyelashes flutter. "But you'll have to excuse the way I look—I just got up a few minutes ago, and the apartment is a mess. But I'll fix us some coffee, and…have you had breakfast?" Aha! The subtle hook.

"Yes, thanks—my lover and I just finished eating." I winked at Tim, who appeared around the corner of the bathroom door just long enough to give me the finger.

"Oh…you have a lover." His voice went flat, as though someone had just slammed the oven door on his soufflé.

"Okay, then," I said, deliberately ignoring both his reaction and his comment. "I'll see you in half an hour."

I hung up, went into the bathroom to say goodbye to Tim and to ask him to call me as soon as he had anything, and left.

*   *   *

Rholfing's apartment was everything I had expected it to be and more. The style was Early Overdone. Some of his ideas were basically good, but he must have been out to corner the glitter-and-spangle market. Gold lame swag curtains covered every window and door, all pulled back with either velvet or rhinestone ties—and in one or two garish instances, both.

He kept apologizing for the mess the place was in, although as I'd expected, there wasn't a gnat's eyebrow out of place. The only hint of overt masculinity in view was a set of barbells inexplicably lying on one side of the foyer. He ushered me in and set me down on one end of an overstuffed love seat (guess who intended to use the other side?) and, still apologizing, whisked out into the kitchen. I could hear the tinkle of fragile cups and good silver in the few microsecond pauses in his chatter.

An obviously new and exorbitantly expensive art book graced the coffee table and I was delighted, as I leaned forward to thumb through it, to find several of the pages uncut.

Rholfing swept back into the room a moment later, bumping the kitchen door closed with his rear-end without missing a step. The tea tray, glinting except for a few rather obvious thumb prints, was heaped high with various croissants, muffins, breakfast rolls, and assorted goodies. Obviously he'd made a record-time sprint to the corner bakery and I probably would have been flattered that he'd gone to the trouble if I didn't recognize trick bait when I saw it.

He set the tray on the coffee table, made a little "hands up" gesture of pleasure, and settled himself, like a bird onto a nest full of eggs, onto the love seat next to me.

"One lump, or two?" he asked, picking up the tiny sugar tongs with a practiced hand.

"None, thanks," I said. "I take it black."

He bravely fought back a slight sneer. With movements that would have done a symphony conductor proud, he poured the coffee. I resisted the temptation to applaud.

"Did you find the photo?" I asked, realizing all the while that I was being more than a little tacky considering the considerable effort he'd gone through to impress me.

"Yes," he said, not quite able to cover his disdain of my obvious lack of sophistication. "I have it in there." He gave an offhand wave toward what I assume to have been the bedroom.

"So tell me a little about you and Bobby," I said, accepting the cup and saucer as gracefully as possible under the circumstances.

Rholfing gave a deep, weltschmerz sigh, dropped two lumps of sugar and a plip of cream into his coffee and stirred, holding the small spoon between thumb and index finger. "What's to tell?" he said, finally. "I'd known him for years—absolutely years— before we ever got together. We lived in the same building. He had this tacky little place— furnished, you know, and I was living in the penthouse suite with a delightful boy named Herb— something. We'd bump into one another from time to time, but never really exchanged…" he made a puckered-lip smile "…words. Croissant?"

He offered me the tray; I took what looked like a miniature prune Danish.

"Soooo," he continued, "then there was this absolutely terrible affair in the building, and I just couldn't stand to stay there any longer. Herb and I moved our separate ways, and that was the last I saw of Bobby for ages. Another croissant?" Licking my fingers—to his raised-eyebrow horror—I shook my head 'no.' "Well, I knew he was a whore even then," Rholfing said, pausing only long enough to take a dainty nibble from something with powdered sugar on it. "But then, about a year ago, while I was 'between engagements,' as they say, I ran into him in one of those sleazy bars I always seem to stumble into when I'm bombed out of my mind. He was almost as drunk as I was—which is saying something—and I asked him home."

Rholfing's eyes misted over, and he sat quiet for the first full moment since I'd come in. "I'll never forget his words," he resumed, his lower lip quivering ever so slightly. "He looked at me, and he said: 'I hear you're a great fuck.' And I said: 'You bet your sweet ass, Charlie,' and we came home together."

He turned quickly to the side, and I could see him dabbing

at his eyes with a handkerchief that had, as in my office, suddenly appeared from nowhere. If I'd suspected there was even a trace of sincerity in his actions, I probably would have felt sorry for him. After a second he took a deep breath and straightened up, regally. "And we were together ever since. Until some sonofabitch killed him."

I reached for another prune Danish. "I don't suppose you have any idea as to who might have done it," I said, "or why. One of the main problems in cases like this is that a lot of times it's a trick the victim's never seen before."

"Oh, Bobby knew him," Rholfing said casually, flicking some powdered sugar off his pant leg. "I always knew when he had somebody special. Not regular special, mind you—not one of those little numbers he'd fuck like clockwork for a week or two until he dumped them—or they dumped him." He rummaged through the diminishing stack of goodies on the tray until he found the one he was looking for, picked it up daintily, and took a mouse-sized bite before placing it on his saucer beside his still-full coffee cup. "I should have known that last morning," he said, ritual completed. "He'd been acting like the cat who ate the canary all the night before, and that morning he had that special look he gets ...got...when a big dick was on the horizon. I knew better than to ask. You never had the privilege of seeing Bobby do one of his 'how-dare-you-accuse-me' numbers. He was a real bastard but...but...I miss him!"

He suddenly burst into tears and threw himself on me, grabbing me so tightly I thought I'd choke. A little awkwardly, I put my arms around his shoulders and patted him on the back. A wrong move, I immediately knew when, with one arm still locked around my neck, his other hand dropped to my crotch.

I pried myself loose as diplomatically as possible and, pleading a kidney problem, excused myself and hastily found my way to the bathroom.

After combing my hair for a minute or two and studying my thumbnail carefully for another minute, I flushed the toilet and returned to the living room. Rholfing was sitting there, drinking coffee and looking regally unconcerned.

"I suppose you'd like the picture now," he said.

"Yeah, that might be a good idea," I said, lamely—being careful not to sit down again. He got up like the Czarina rising from her throne, and undulated into the bedroom, to return a second later with a Polaroid picture of a good-looking young guy, totally nude, in what might best be described as a "suggestive pose." Rholfing hadn't been kidding when he said Bobby McDermott had certain striking resemblances to a horse.

"I thought you'd like one that showed off his best features," Rholfing said. "More coffee?"

"Uhhh, no, thanks," I said, forcing myself to stop looking at the photo and putting it in my shirt pocket.

"Is there anything else I can get you?" he asked, coquettishly, at the same time giving a not-too-subtle glance toward the bedroom. This guy apparently had difficulty with the more complex words of the English language—such as "no."

"Ah, no thanks. I've really got to get going. Thanks for the pic…I mean, thanks for the coffee. I'll call you as soon as I find out anything." Somehow, I bumbled my way to the door.

"*Do* that," Rholfing said, just a little sarcastically, I thought. And when he closed the door behind me, it was just a little more forcefully than necessary. As a matter of fact, it was just this side of a slam.

*   *   *

I went home to shower and shave and change clothes, did some laundry, then went to the office and farted around for awhile with a crossword puzzle, hoping to hear from Tim.

In a way, I suppose I was trying to avoid thinking about just what in hell I'd gotten myself into. What I thought would be a quick case-open, case-closed affair looked like it could be something I wasn't sure I really wanted to get involved in. A simple drug overdose is one thing; suicide another, but murder—make that probably six murders?

After what seemed like four days, I glanced at my watch and saw it was only 2:00, so I decided to go back to Hughie's. Bud had mentioned somebody named Tessie who might have known Bobby. Back when I'd been assuming Bobby had OD'd on drugs, it didn't really matter who knew him or who didn't. Now it mattered. Maybe Bud had Tessie's phone number. Besides, now that I had McDermott's photo, it might help find out if anyone else there knew him.

Walking into Hughie's in the daytime is always like entering a coal mine—and the brighter the day outside, the stronger the contrast. The day's heat was suddenly replaced by the clammy, stale-beer-smelling dampness of the air conditioning. The 25-watt bulbs behind the bar were not materially aided by three or four flickering candles in those God-awful net-stockinged colored bowls set out on the booths along the wall. I was, as usual, temporarily blinded. As I stumbled my way to the bar, I bumped rather abruptly into a well-rounded ass in tight Levi's.

"Sorry," I mumbled.

"Twenty-five a feel, Mack," was the gracious reply from somewhere in the darkness beneath what I dimly made out to be a cowboy hat.

"You take Master Card?" I asked, and reached out for an empty barstool. My eyes were now becoming accustomed to the gloom, and I could see five or six forms slouched at various stools along the bar. Most of the forms, when I could make out their faces, I recognized as regulars.

Bud cut off a muttered conversation with one of them at the far end of the bar, waved, and automatically reached into the cooler for a glass. He pulled me a dark and brought it over. I handed him a wadded bill I'd found that morning at the bottom of my pants pocket.

"Planning to make a spit-ball?" he asked as he unwadded the bill. I just grinned.

"Hey, Bud, remember I was asking you about a guy named Bobby McDermott?"

"Yeah—but like I said, nobody's much on names around here. Did you find Tessie?"

"Nope, I didn't get a chance to come back. I got tied up."

"So I see from the bags under your eyes. You S&M types

are all alike."

We both laughed, and I reached into my shirt pocket for the Polaroid photo. "This is the guy I'm interested in." I handed the photo to Bud, who reached under the bar for a flashlight to enable him to see. He snapped on the light and let out a long, low whistle.

"Holy shit!" he said. "No wonder you're lookin' for him! If you find him, can I have seconds?"

I didn't tell him Bobby McDermott was no longer in any condition to give firsts, let alone seconds. But before I had a chance make any reply at all, I felt a dark form beside me, and turned to see Cowboy had moved down the bar to look at the picture. In the reflection of Bud's flashlight, and with my eyes a little better accustomed to what little light there was in the place, I could see Cowboy was definitely not one of the regulars. I momentarily was tempted to say something brilliant, like: "What's a guy like you doing in a place like this?" But because it *was* a place like this, I knew good and well what he was doing in it.

"Lemme see, Bud," Cowboy said, holding out a large, un-calloused hand.

"Recognize him?" I asked Bud, who continued to stare at the photo.

"I dunno—I haven't gotten up to the face yet."

"I said '*Lemme see*,' Bud," Cowboy repeated, hand still calmly extended.

Bud shot him a dirty look, flicked off the flashlight, and handed the photo to Cowboy, who tilted it toward the nearest dim light. He nodded silently.

"Know him?" I asked.

"Who wants to know?" he replied, not belligerently.

"*I* want to know," I said. "Didn't you just hear me ask?"

"You vice?"

I pulled out my wallet to show him it had no police badge. He seemed to relax a bit.

"What's it worth to you?" he asked, in his best hustler voice.

"Would you believe, my undying gratitude?"

The flicker of a grin crossed his face like summer light-ning."What you looking for him for?"

"I'm not looking for him," I said. "I know where he is—I just want to find out some more about him."

"Then why don't you ask him?"

"I wish I could," I said.

Cowboy stared at me. "He in trouble?" Again, I could feel him tense up.

"Not any more," I said. "He's dead."

"Oh." The voice was like a little boy's. When he spoke again, it was neither a little boy's nor a hardened hustler's. "Yeah, I know… knew…him." He gave a long sigh. "Buy me a beer?"

Now, I have pretty strong moral scruples against buying hustlers drinks, but in Cowboy's case, I was willing to make an exception. After all, I rationalized, I could write it off my income tax as a business expense—particularly if he could give me some information about Bobby McDermott. And what the hell…he didn't ask for champagne. I drained my glass, signaled to Bud, and raised two fingers. He nodded and moved off to draw two.

In the pause, I took stock of Cowboy. There was a lot there to take stock of. Six-three, Levi's, boots, Levi's jacket open to the navel, no shirt. Nice chest, with just a patch of hair bridging the space between his nicely-shaped pecs and trailing down suggestively toward his crotch. A very respectable basket and an ass to match.

Bud returned with the beers, and Cowboy gestured thanks as he raised his glass and took a long, Adam's-apple-bobbing drink. Then he set the glass down and pushed his hat to the back of his head, exposing a beautiful head of wavy black hair. He hooked his free thumb under his belt and raised one boot to the bar rail. Turning to me, he leaned against the bar with one elbow. This kid had it down to a tee. All he needed was a pack of Marlboros.

He pulled out a pack of Marlboros, tapped one out of the pack with an index finger, and lit up with cupped hands. When he'd done just about everything butch he could think of at the moment, he took a long drag, blew it out one corner of his mouth slowly, and said: "What happened to Bobby?"

"That's what I'm trying to find out," I said.

Cowboy took the cigarette out of his mouth and set it in the ashtray in front of him.

"Thought you said you weren't a cop?" he said, watching my face closely.

"I'm not; I'm a private investigator."

Cowboy reached out and tamped the cigarette out in the ashtray, then looked at me again. "What you want to know?"

"Well, for starters, my name's Dick—what's yours?"

"Tex."

"Yeah, I know. But what's your *name*?"

He grinned, and once again I could see him relax—a lot further this time. The thumb came out of the belt, the boot off the rail, and he leaned forward to put both elbows on the bar.

"Phil," he said, and gave me a natural smile, showing about 72 of the whitest, most even teeth I'd ever seen.

"I like it better than Tex," I said, returning the smile. "So, how well did you know Bobby?"

"Not all that well, I guess—but then how well does anybody know anybody in this business? We made it a couple of times when business was slow, and we turned a couple of tricks together. Mostly, we'd just stand around and bullshit."

"Did he come in here often?"

"I don't know. Probably not. He had a lover—some possessive little fag from what I hear—who kept him on a pretty short leash. You got a lover?" I could feel his eyes on mine and I looked up from my beer to find I was right. I stared at him for a few seconds, and felt the old electric current flowing between us.

"Not at the moment. Why'd you ask?"

He shrugged and grinned. "Just wondered." He dropped his glance into his nearly empty glass. "Be interested in a little action?" he asked, almost shyly.

Is the pope catholic? I thought. Damn, why did he have to be a hustler? "Sorry, Phil…I don't pay for it. Besides, we haven't finished talking about Bobby yet."

"So I don't always charge," he said. "You got someplace we can go…talk?"

"My office is a couple blocks from here," I said, feeling myself weakening.

"Great. I do some of my best talking in offices." He drained the rest of his beer, put his glass down, and pushed himself away from the bar with both hands. "Let's go."

I set my beer down without finishing it, and followed him out the door.

*　*　*

By the time I'd closed and locked the office door, Tex/Phil had taken his shirt off and tossed it in the general direction of the chair by the window. Taking one look at that flawless, muscled torso convinced me that there *has* to be a God.

I started unbuttoning my shirt, but Tex/Phil panthered his way across the room and stood inches away. I couldn't stop staring at his pecs and those fantastic, perfect round nipples.

"Here, let me do that for you," he said, and reached out to push my hands aside. His face was less than 6 inches from mine, so I used my now-free hands to grab him by the back of the neck and pull him to me. He opened his mouth slightly, and I felt his tongue slip past my lips. I made a little whimper and sucked on it like it was the nipple on a baby's bottle.

After a few minutes, we came up for air and finished undressing, throwing clothes into a general pile in the center of the room. When he finally slipped his shorts down and I got a glimpse of that monster sticking straight up from between his legs, I swore I'd died and gone to heaven. Sliding my own shorts down, Tex/Phil gave an appreciative whistle. "Not *bad!*" he said, and pushed me back onto the couch. I plopped down onto the cushion and Tex/Phil towered over me.

"You like to fuck?" he asked.

"Shit, yes," I said. "But I don't get fucked very often—and especially not with a donkey-dong like that."

"Who asked?" he murmured and knelt with his face between

my legs. I closed my eyes as the indescribable warm wetness slowly engulfed me, withdrew, and then consumed me even more. Then, suddenly, he stopped and pushed my knees together with his own. He straddled me and, grasping me firmly, slowly lowered himself in position. "Jee-ZUS" he hissed through clenched teeth, but kept on moving lower until I felt his hips resting on me.

I opened my eyes to see his magnificent column only inches from my lips, and I instinctively leaned forward.

"Like it?" he asked.

I pulled my head away long enough to look up at him and say: "Ride 'em, Cowboy!" And he did.

When, after what must have been three of the most wonderful days of my life, Tex/Phil finally got off my lap and I struggled valiantly to get my head out of the clouds and back to reality.

"I hate to bring up the subject of business—my business, that is," I said as I struggled to my feet to get a cup of water from the cooler, "but I really need to find out some more about Bobby McDermott."

"Sure," Tex/Phil said, grinning and running a big hand over his sweat-beaded chest.

"When's the last time you saw him?"

Tex/Phil reached down and rummaged through his Levi's, looking for cigarettes and matches. Finding them, he tossed the Levi's back onto the pile of our mixed clothes and lit up. He took a long drag and eased himself back on the sofa. "Ummmmm… 'bout a week and a half ago, I guess. A Tuesday night. We ran into each other at the 'Macho'."

"Did he pick up a trick?"

"Nope, 's a matter of fact, he didn't. He came in around nine, I guess it was, just for a beer. He was alone, but said he was on his way to a big date."

"A score?"

"I don't think so. He didn't say for sure, but he mentioned something about it being a guy he'd been after for years."

"Anything else? A name, maybe?"

"Nope." He looked around for an ashtray and I indicated one on top of the filing cabinet. He got up and walked over to it like some sleek jungle cat. Picking up the ashtray, he returned to the sofa and sat beside me.

"Did he mention where he was going to meet the guy?"

Tex/Phil pursed his lips and wrinkled his brow, obviously searching his memory. Suddenly, the lips unpursed, the wrinkles smoothed, and a light practically went on in his eyes. "Yeah. Yeah. Said the dude had rented a hotel room someplace up the street. The El Cordoba, I think."

"Why the hotel room?" I asked. "Was the guy from out of town?"

Tex/Phil shrugged. "Or married," he said. "Or a closet case. Or any one of a dozen reasons. You know the hotels in that area—they aren't exactly the kind that draws the business convention crowd. Most of 'em will rent by the hour."

I understood.

"Any of that help you?" he asked after a couple minutes of silence in which he smoked his cigarette and I sifted through the few facts I had about Bobby McDermott, trying to find some direction they might lead me next.

"Yeah," I said, reaching out and putting one hand on his bare, hard-muscled leg. "Thanks, Phil."

Tex/Phil stubbed his cigarette out in the ashtray and set it on the floor. He covered my hand with his and gave me another dazzling grin. "Care for a rematch?" he asked.

I cared.

CHAPTER 3

The phone rang just as Tex/Phil was lighting another cigarette. I managed to gather enough strength to lift the receiver off the hook.

"Hardesty," I said, in a voice that belonged to someone else.

"Yeah, that's who I called." Tim's voice sounded a little tired, but cheerful. "How goes the battle?"

I wondered how he knew. "Everything's fine," I said.

"You sure you're okay?" Tim asked, with a note of real concern that made me feel just a little guilty. "You sound funny."

"It's nothing," I said. "I just had something in my throat."

"Anyone I know?"

"Thank you and good night, Henny Youngman," I said, glancing at Tex/Phil, who gave me a knowing grin. "So what did you find out?"

"Now look," Tim said in a conspiratorial tone, "I'm at a public phone—it's my coffee break, so I'll have to talk fast. The…you got a pencil?"

I moved around to the back of my desk and dug through the top drawer for a pencil and some paper. "Yeah," I said, hooking the phone between my right ear and shoulder.

"Okay. Here goes. Victims, in order of discovery: Rogers—Alan Rogers. Age 33. 27 Partridge Place, Apartment D as in 'dog.' Identified by who I'll bet was his lover, Gary Miller—who I'd love to spend a quiet night or two consoling. Rogers had two arrests, both for drunk driving. Family disown, apparently.

"Harriman, Gene. Age 29. 7986 Bellwether—that's a residential area, so I assume it's a house. Identified by his 'roommate,' Mike Sibalitch. One arrest, apparently an entrapment—the usual 'Lewd and Lascivious Conduct' shit—two years ago. Two brothers, one living in Miami, the other in the Navy overseas.

"Granger, Arthur. Age 40. 10438 Mercer Drive. Lived alone. The body was identified by a Martin Bell—the one I told you got hysterical and said too much. Bell lives in the Comstock Apartments—I don't have the address. No police record on Granger. Family lives in Ohio.

"Barker, Cletus—went by the name of Clete. Age 33. 4427 West Avondale, Apartment 5-J. Identified by his 'roommate' Bill Elers—the one I told you I've seen in the bars. No police record, no known family.

"Klein, Arnold. 36. His dad's the one who went into the 'I have no son' routine, even though he did deign to identify the body. 6130 Kessner. No record. Lived with two other guys, both of whom were out of town when it happened.

"Number six was your friend, McDermott. No record, and you know all the other information.

"That's about it. You get it all?"

"Yeah," I said, dropping the pencil and shaking my wrist to get rid of a bad case of writer's cramp I always develop when I try to write too fast and have to worry about making it legible at the same time. "Except for two things: where, and when?"

"Oh, shit, Dick Tracy! Hold on." I heard the phone being put down and the shuffling of papers, accompanied by a string of muttered oaths. I picked up the pencil when I heard him pick up the phone. "Here goes: Rogers, Harriman, Barker, and Granger were all found at home. Klein was found behind some bushes in Davis Park, about 75 feet from the most popular tearoom in the area. Dates are…" again the shuffling of papers "…Rogers, May 17; Harriman, May 23; Granger, June 10; Barker, June 12; Klein, June 15—our friend must have had a busy week, assuming they weren't all just your average, run-of-the-mill kill-yourself-with-cyanide suicides."

"And McDermott?" I asked.

Tim sounded puzzled. "I thought you knew all about him. He was found…ah…July 6, Room 414 of the El Cordoba Hotel on Main."

The mention of the El Cordoba Hotel gave me that old sinking sensation in my stomach, and a quick glance at the calendar verified that July 6 fell on a Wednesday. Bobby's beer with Phil had probably been his last.

"Are you still there?" Tim asked, bringing me back to reality.

"I'm still here," I said.

"Good. Can I go back to work, now, Massah? I've got to tear

up these damn notes and swallow them or do something to get rid of them before I go back to the office. Or maybe I can roll them up and shove them…"

"Ah-ah-ahhh!" I cautioned. "Let's not get testy. I'll give you a call at home tomorrow and see if there isn't some way I can repay you for your able assistance. You'd make a great Number One Son."

"Fuck you, too, Charlie Chan," Tim laughed, and hung up.

I quickly scanned my notes to make sure they were, indeed, legible. They were, though just barely. I then turned my attention back to Tex/ Phil.

"Phil, think hard about the last time you saw Bobby. Is there anything you can think of that you didn't tell me? Anything else Bobby might have said about the guy he had the date with?"

He thought a minute, then shook his head. "Afraid not," he said, then added, "except he did say something about being surprised the guy would look him up after what happened."

"After what happened?" I asked.

Phil shrugged. "He didn't say—must have crossed the guy somehow."

"Is there anything else you can think of?" I urged.

"Nope."

"You're sure?"

"I'm sure. Man," he said, still sprawled out with one arm dangling off the sofa and onto the floor, "You're something else!" He wore a broad grin.

"I bet you say that to all your tricks," I said, moving to the pile of clothes on the floor and reaching for my shorts.

He grinned. "Shit, no! I usually don't even have to talk to them. It's just that I never met a real, live detective before. It's kind of exciting." He got up from the sofa and joined me, pawing through the piled clothes.

"And speaking of tricks," he said, stepping into his briefs, "I'd best get out there and go to work."

We finished dressing in silence, and when we were both fully clothed, Tex/Phil came over and extended his hand. "Any time you want another rematch," he said, "you just look me up.

Compliments of the house."

"And whenever you want something looked into, you know where to find me," I said.

We exchanged grins and a bear hug, and with that Tex/Phil hiked up his jeans, plunked his hat at a sexy angle on the back of his head and went out the door.

*   *   *

By the time I'd straightened out the office—which consisted mainly of emptying Tex/Phil's ashtray and resisting the temptation to get a few drags out of the butts still salvable, typing my notes to be sure I had everything straight, and checking the phone book for the numbers of the deceased and/or their friends/lovers Tim had mentioned, it was close to 5. I went home, defrosted a steak and made a salad, then spent the rest of the night staring glassy-eyed at the boob tube.

I'd just gotten to bed, around 11, when the phone rang. "Mr. Hardesty?" I'd have recognized Rholfing's simper anywhere. So much for an unlisted phone number. I forced myself not to ask what the hell he wanted and how he'd gotten my number. After all, like it or not, he was my bread and butter for the moment, and the thought flashed briefly through my head that Tex/Phil's and my professions were not really all that different: we both had to get into bed—Tex/ Phil literally, me figuratively—with people we'd just as soon not.

"Yes, Mr. Rholfing," I said, assuming my most businesslike voice. "What can I do for you?" As soon as I said it, I knew he was going to jump on it with both feet, and I could have bitten my tongue off.

Sure enough, there was a girlish giggle, followed by the inevitable reply: "What did you have in mind?"

Nothing, buddy, believe me—nothing!

When I made no reply there was a four or five second pause. His voice, when he resumed talking, was all business. "I'm really sorry to trouble you at home, Mr. Hardesty," he'd gotten the message on that, too, I was glad to see, "but I couldn't find your phone number, though I was sure you'd given it to me." I hadn't. "You really should talk to those people at your answering service. *Snip-py*! Anyway, I have this dear friend at the phone company who managed to get it for me."

I made a mental note to call the phone company in the morning and chew the asses off a couple of supervisors. "So how can I help you?" Shit! I did it again! Fortunately, he let this one drop.

"Well, I suppose it's not really that important, but I rather expected to hear from you this evening to let me know what you'd found out. You know, when you're all alone in the world like I am, without a soul except for old Ass-Face in Fort Worth, you're naturally curious about who killed your lover. And I'd be more than happy to help you out in any way I can."

I'll just bet you would, I thought. "Well, that's really nice of you, Mr. Rholfing," I said, "but everything's pretty much under control. I've got a few leads I'm following up on, but I really didn't want to bother you until I have something solid to report." I got out of bed as I talked and, trailing the phone with me (thank God for the 15-foot extension cord) went into the kitchen to get my billfold from the coffee bar.

"Well, if there is anything I can ever do…"

I fished the list out of the billfold and ironed it out on the bar with my hand. "As a matter of fact," I said, "while I've got you on the phone…I've come up with a few names I wonder if you might be familiar with." I read him the list of victims and their lovers/friends, without mentioning their connection with the case. "Any of them ring a bell?"

After a short pause, during which I could picture him beetling his plucked little brows, he said: "Granger. Definitely Granger. What did you say his first name was?"

"Arthur."

"Oh." He sounded definitely let down. "No, I must have been thinking of Stewart Granger. I just loved him in 'King Solomon's Mines,' didn't you? But there is someone else—a Rogers?" If he came up with "Ginger," I swore to myself that I'd hang up.

"Alan Rogers."

"Alan Rogers…Alan Rogers…yes, I definitely know that name. And Barker… Festus, was it?"

"Cletus…Clete."

"Clete Barker! Yes, that one too. As a matter of fact, they all sound familiar, but I'm absolutely horrible with names. I just call everybody 'Darling'—it makes it so much easier. But let me think…Of course! Of course I recognize them, now. The police asked me if Bobby knew them…or most of them, I think. I'm afraid I wasn't exactly in my best form that day. Still, some of them do ring a bell, if only I could remember. Who are these people, anyway? Some of Bobby's tricks?" He let out a small, dramatic gasp. "Do you suppose they could be *suspects*?"

"I doubt that very much," I said honestly. "As to whether any of them were Bobby's tricks, I couldn't say—but I'll be sure to check that out. I just thought you might know some of them."

"I really do wish I could help you, but as I say, I'm just terrible at remembering names. I remember…shall we say, *other* things?" He giggled—just a tad hysterically, I thought.

"Well," I said, in an effort to cut off the giggles if nothing else, "try to remember if you can, and call me at the office" (I hoped he got that, but doubted it) "as soon as you do. It might be important."

"Oh, I will. I will! Just as soon as I can think of it. I've really enjoyed talking with you, Mr. Hardesty. It's so nice to have someone you can really talk to, don't you think?"

"Yes; that's what my lover always says."

"Oh…yes…I'd forgotten you were married. Well, I hope I didn't *interrupt* anything…" This time it was a snigger.

"Not at all," I assured him. "We were just getting ready for bed." I don't like lying, but having an imaginary lover was going to be a necessity as long as Rholfing was on the prowl.

"Well, good night, then. And you will be sure to keep in touch?" Again the seductive tone.

"Of course. And you be sure to call my office whenever you remember anything. If I'm not there, just leave a message with the service, and I'll get back to you. Good night." I hung up before he could drag the conversation out any longer.

I turned out the light, went back to bed, and mentally smoked a cigarette. Imagining you're smoking a cigarette is sort of like masturbation—it's better than nothing, but not much.

There was, I was sure now, some definite connection between Bobby McDermott and the other victims—something other than the fact of their being gay. And if there was a link, that pretty much ruled out a random serial killer, which might make finding out who did it a little easier. It still meant that I was, by trying to find out who killed Bobby McDermott, in effect out to solve six murders. That disturbing hunch I was getting into something a lot more than I'd bargained for returned, and I was now more than sure that I wasn't too happy about it.

I could have spent the rest of the night pondering the possibilities, but decided to take a tip from Rhett Butler's girlfriend and worry about it tomorrow. Having made that decision, I tossed and turned for all of ten seconds before falling into a deep and Technicolor-dreamed sleep.

*   *   *

The alarm clock in my head went off at exactly six thirty, as usual. I laid in bed for a few minutes while my thoughts and various parts of my consciousness wandered in from wherever they'd been overnight and took their places in my mind. When most of them were present and accounted for, I got up, showered, shaved, brushed my teeth, and went through all the exciting rituals that make up a morning. I'd remembered to set the timer on the coffee maker before I'd gone to bed, so there was a hot pot waiting for me when I finally staggered into the kitchen.

The first order of business, once I was fairly certain I could talk coherently, was to try to reach the numbers of the room-mates/lovers Tim had given me. It was about 8:10, and I might have a chance to catch some of them before they left for work.

There were three Gary Millers in the phone book, but only one on Partridge Place. Gary Miller was the one Tim had been so taken with, and when the phone was answered on the first ring, I could understand why. The voice was the stuff of which wet dreams are made. "Good morning. Gary Miller here."

"Mr. Miller," I responded, hoping my voice sounded one tenth as intriguing as his. "Good morning. My name is Hardesty, and I'm a private investigator. I'd like to talk to you about your friend Alan Rogers."

"Alan is dead."

"I know, and I'm sorry for your loss. That's what I wanted to talk to you about."

"Who do you represent?" The voice, while still sexy, had a definite no-nonsense tone. "The insurance company? If so, you'll have to contact Alan's parents."

"No, it's nothing like that, I can assure you," I said. "I'm doing some work on a case for a client and I have reason to believe that you might know some of the people Mr. Rogers knew, who in turn are connected with the case. It all sounds pretty complicated over the phone, but it is rather important or I never would have bothered you. Is there any way we could get together for a few minutes, in person?"

His sexy voice was considerably more relaxed. "Yes, I guess we could do that, though I can tell you now I didn't know that many of Alan's friends. We're doing a shoot today at the beach, and I'll probably be tied up until around nine tonight. If you want to come by then for a few minutes, it's okay."

"I really appreciate that. Twenty-seven Partridge Place, Apartment D," I said, by way of verification. "I'll look forward to seeing you. So long." But before I could hang up, Miller's voice caught me.

"I hope you're not trying to imply some sinister motivation behind Alan's death, because I can assure you there was none."

"Not at all," I lied, wondering how he could be so sure, "but we can talk about that when I see you. Okay?"

"Okay," he said, and hung up.

There was no listing for Mike Sibalitch, but Gene Harriman, the second victim, was in the book. I dialed, let the phone ring four times, and was just about to hang up when I heard the phone being picked up on the other end. A few second's pause was followed by a very sleepy-sounding: "Yeah?"

"Mike Sibalitch?" I asked.

Another long pause, then an equally sleepy "Yeah."

"I'm sorry if I woke you. My name is Hardesty. I'm a private investigator, and I'd like to talk to you about Gene Harriman."

"What about Gene?"

"To be honest with you, Mr. Sibalitch, I'm not quite sure. But I'm working on a case and I think that somehow Mr. Harriman might possibly be connected."

From the pauses that loomed between my statements and his, I got the feeling that I was talking with someone on the other side of the moon, and that there was a built-in time delay. Finally, there was a reply. "Look, Mr. Harsty, I work nights and I'm really in no condition to talk right now. I'd be very willing to talk to you about Gene but, frankly, right now I'm too zonked to even know my own name. Could you call back this afternoon about five? I should be pretty much together by then."

"Sure," I said. "Again I'm sorry to have disturbed your sleep. I'll give you a call la…" There was a click on the other end, then a dial tone. I took the hint and hung up.

None of the Bells listed in the book had the address Tim had given me for Arthur Granger, and there was no 'Martin Bell' listed either. But there was an 'M. Bell,' and I decided to take a chance on it.

A woman's voice answered: "Bell residence."

If a woman answers, hang up, I thought. But since I had her on the line… "Good morning," I said. "Is Martin Bell in?"

"No, sir. He'd be at work. I'm his housekeeper."

Phew! Lucked out! "Is there some way I might reach Mr. Bell at work?"

"Oh, yes, sir. Mr. Bell'll be at the gallery."

I waited for a little more information, and when it was not forthcoming, I felt it necessary to fill in the lull in the conversation. "Which gallery is that, again?"

"Why, Bell, Book, & Candle!" She sounded genuinely surprised that I had to be told—almost as though I'd asked her in which direction the sun rose.

I fumbled for the pencil and pad I try to keep by the phone but usually wander off with, and couldn't find it. Well, I doubted I could forget anything as campily predictable as 'Bell, Book, & Candle.' I wouldn't be particularly surprised to find that there was a Mr. Book and a Mr. Candle there, too. Maybe I was just getting jaded.

"Well, thank you very much," I said in what I hoped was a pleasant-enough tone. It doesn't pay to alienate housekeepers. "Have a good day."

I hung up and took a big swig of coffee, which was by now not even lukewarm. I got up, dumped it into the sink, and poured another cup from the pot.

Neither Cletus Barker nor Bill Elers were listed in the directory. I'd have to find some other way of contacting Bill Elers. Arnold Klein was listed, but there was no answer.

Finding Bell, Book, & Candle's number was no problem, and the phone was answered on the first ring. "Bell, Book, & Candle." The voice was smooth, professional, and controlled; definitely not the kind of voice one would associate with hysterics.

"May I speak to Martin Bell?" I asked.

"This is he. How may I serve you?"

"Mr. Bell, my name is Hardesty, and I was hoping you might spare me a couple of minutes to talk about Arthur Granger."

"Are you with the police, Mr. Hardesty?" The voice had just a trace less smoothness, but the control showed more.

"No, sir. I'm a private investigator, and Mr. Granger may have some connection to a case I'm working on."

"Arthur? I don't mean to be rude, Mr. Hardesty, but I cannot imagine Arthur having anything to do with anything that might involve a private investigator." Still more control, heavily laced with suspicion.

"It would really be easier to talk in person, Mr. Bell," I said. "Would you have some time today to see me?"

There was a slight pause, then: "Yes, I suppose. Today should be a light day. You may come by any time."

"Thank you, sir," I said. "I should be there within the hour."

"Until then," he said, and hung up.

An hour would give me just about enough time. I finished my coffee, rinsed out the cup, got dressed, and left.

* * *

The housekeeper had referred to it as a "gallery," though it sounded more like a head shop for gay warlocks. I was therefore mildly surprised and impressed to find that Bell, Book, & Candle was a rather nice little art gallery just off the stretch of Brookhaven known as "Decorators' Row." Bell, or whomever it was who owned the place, had made maximum use of a minimum of space without giving the impression of clutter. Heavy on modern paintings, but with a good mixture of sketches, etchings, and small sculpture.

When I first walked in—noting the neatly lettered "To the Trade" sign on the door—I thought the place was empty of people. But as I walked over to admire a small, ebony figurine which turned out to be a faun's head, I heard a pleasant "May I help you?"

Standing no more than five feet from me—I had no idea where he came from—was a tall, slender man with once-red hair and enormous jowls which gave him the look of a friendly beagle.

"Mr. Bell?" I asked, hoping my shock at having him suddenly appear from nowhere didn't show. I extended my hand. "Dick Hardesty."

We shook hands, and Bell gave a fleeting little smile, in which both ends of his mouth raised upward and disappeared into his jowls.

"Shall we go into my office?" he said, gesturing with a palm-up sweep of his hand to a small alcove neatly hidden from the rest of the gallery, but with a view of the front door. So that's where he'd come from!

Seating himself behind a small but obviously very expensive antique desk, he motioned me to one of three small chairs of the same wood as the desk. Leaning forward, his elbows on the edge of the desk, his hands folded as if in prayer, he stared at me for a full ten seconds before speaking.

"I'm really not sure why you're here, Mr. Hardesty, or how I can help you—or even if I should be talking with you at all. As I mentioned to you on the phone, I have no idea how Arthur could have anything to do with whatever it is you are engaged in. Arthur's private life is not a matter for public airing."

"I know Mr. Granger was gay, if that's what's worrying you," I said. "My client is gay, I'm gay—it's all strictly a family affair. It's just that I think there might have been some sort of link between my client and Mr. Granger. What it is, I haven't any idea; that's what I'd like to find out. I'd very much appreciate any help you can give me. And I promise I'm not out to cause any trouble for you, for Mr. Granger, or for anyone else."

Running the tip of his tongue quickly over the inner rim of his lower lip, Bell pushed himself back from the edge of his desk to settle back in his chair.

"What is it you'd like to know?"

I allowed myself to relax a little, too, being careful as I crossed my legs not to kick the desk in the process.

"I don't know what your relationship was with Mr. Granger …" I began.

"Friends," he interrupted, again giving me that fleeting smile. "Friends."

"…or how close your friendship may have been. But would you know if Mr. Granger knew a man named Bobby McDermott?"

Bell pursed his lips and looked up toward the ceiling for a moment. "No," he said finally, "I'm not aware that Arthur knew anyone by that name. At least I never met him or heard Arthur mention his name."

"How about Clete Barker? Gene Harriman? Arnold Klein? Alan Rogers?"

Bell looked at me strangely. "Why, that's peculiar," he said. "The police asked me if Arthur knew an Alan Rogers or a Gene Harriman. I told them 'no.' They didn't mention the other two, though."

That, I thought, wasn't surprising—Granger was the third victim; Barker and Klein were still alive when the police talked to Bell. Apparently, they hadn't thought it worth checking with him again.

"Do you know if Mr. Granger knew Clete Barker or Arnold Klein, then?" I asked.

Bell hadn't taken his eyes off me. "I don't believe so," he said. "Perhaps you could tell me why you and the police are asking about the same people?"

A good question. I hoped I could come up with a good answer. "It's rather complicated," I said, "and my client has asked me not to go into detail, but the police are apparently investigating a related case involving some of the same individuals."

I could see Bell stiffen. "Are you implying that Arthur was involved in some sort of illegal activity?"

"Not at all," I hastened to reassure him. "I have no indication whatever that Mr. Granger did anything illegal; I'm merely trying to establish some sort of link between the four men I've mentioned, and believe that Mr. Granger might have been aware of what that link may be."

Bell relaxed again, and I thought it best to change the subject.

"Do you happen to know the cause of Mr. Granger's death?" I asked.

Bell's eyes were still riveted to my own, and I could see water gathering in the folds of his lower lids. When he blinked, a tear began to move down one of the crevices in his face. He didn't even appear to notice it, at first.

"Arthur was only 40 years old, but heart problems run in his family," he said. "His father died at 38, his grandfather at 50."

"And that's what the police told you...a heart attack?" I asked.

"The police told me nothing," he said with a sigh. Taking a deep breath, Bell sat up straight and made an almost-unconscious swiping gesture along his mouth line with one index finger, catching the tear just before it reached his chin.

"Did they mention the possibility of suicide?" I asked.

Bell stiffened in his chair as though I'd slapped him.

"They asked if he might have had a reason to take his own life," he said. "But I told them that was ridiculous. Arthur was a devout Catholic; the very idea of suicide would be inconceivable to him."

"I'm sorry if I upset you," I said sincerely. "You did not see the death certificate, I assume?"

Bell struggled to maintain his composure. "Are you telling me the police believe Arthur committed suicide? How could they—how *dare* they—assume such a thing? I told them about his heart condition."

"If it is any consolation to you," I said, "I don't believe that Mr. Granger committed suicide."

Bell leaned forward in his chair. "Then what are you saying? Why are you asking about these other people? Why would the police ask me about them if they thought Arthur killed himself?"

I'd gotten myself on very shaky ground and was looking desperately for a way to avoid creating any more problems.

"Please don't leap to any conclusions, Mr. Bell," I said, hopefully reassuringly. "It's just that we both know the police are sometimes less than thorough when it comes to investigating the deaths of gay men. I'm simply trying to determine if Mr. Granger had any association with the men I've mentioned to you; perhaps resolving that issue may lead to more concrete facts."

Bell did not look completely convinced.

"Perhaps you could tell me a little more about Mr. Granger," I suggested, hoping to divert Bell from the path his questions were inevitably taking him.

It seemed to work. Bell took a few deep breaths and sat back into his chair.

"We were very good friends, Arthur and I," he began. "We were…more than friends… once, for a short time very long ago, but we always remained close."

He reached out to open a small, oriental box on one corner of his desk. He took out a thin brown cigarillo and offered me one with a nod of his head and a raised eyebrow. I shook my head 'no,' and he closed the box, then reached into his pocket for a gold lighter. He took a long, slow drag, exhaling the smoke in a thin, straight line. I had to force myself not to lean forward and inhale it.

"Arthur was, as far as most people were concerned, not particularly likable. He used crudity and crassness as a wall against the world. But for whatever reason, he was one of the highlights of my life," he continued, one hand in his lap, the other holding the cigarillo an inch or so from his lips. "He was from Ohio—but I suppose you knew that—and had a rotten childhood. As a result, Arthur could never keep away from the truck-driver types. How we ever got together, I'll never know. But we did. It was just that we were too different—or perhaps too much alike." He smiled and reached into a desk drawer for an ashtray.

"If Arthur had one fault, it was his fascination for ultra-butch types without a brain in their heads. I tried to warn him, God knows. I'd beg him to stop going to those S&M places but he'd just laugh. He said he felt safer there than he did just walking down the street. It was all just a game, he'd say."

He took another long drag on the cigarillo, then stubbed it out in the ashtray, half-smoked. He let the smoke from his last drag out slowly, so that it curled up from the entire width of his mouth, as though his tongue were on fire.

"Arthur was responsible for my getting this shop, actually," he said, looking into the ashtray. "About six years ago, my parents died and I went back to Missouri to clear up their affairs. My father had a small business there, and I remained in Missouri for nearly three years. Arthur and I kept in close contact, of course. Then, about three years ago, he went through some sort of trauma—he never would discuss it with me—and pleaded with me to come back here. Which I did. I sold my father's business and bought this shop. I'm very glad I did, really."

"You didn't live together, though?" I asked.

"Only for the shortest of times, shortly after we first met, but our lifestyles were really just too different, and it never would have worked out. We got along much better by not living together.

"He carried my name in his wallet on one of those 'In case of emergency, call...' cards. I carried his. And one bright Tuesday morning I got a call from the police with the request that I come to the morgue." Again, I could see his eyes water, and he turned his head away quickly to wipe at them with a thumb and index finger, as if trying to pinch them off at the source.

Finally, he took another deep breath and turned to me again, trying to smile and failing.

"I'd never seen a dead body before—my parents died in a plane crash at sea and their bodies were never recovered—let alone been to a morgue. Dreadful, dreadful place. I certainly wouldn't recommend it as a Sunday outing with the wife and kiddies." He gave me a quick, very weak smile. "I pride myself on being a man of considerable composure, but I'm afraid I behaved rather badly. From the attitude of the police when they contacted me, I assumed the worst; that he'd been murdered by one of those cretins he was so pathetically attracted to, and I was angry with him for being so stupid. Silly, but I didn't even consider it being his heart at first. I'm afraid I said some things I shouldn't have. Then they showed me the body—his face, anyway—and there was not a mark on him. He was very pale, of course, and his lips were a very strange shade of blue; I suppose that's how all corpses must look. I knew then it was his heart but, unfortunately, things said cannot be unsaid.

"There was a very nice young man there who took me into his office after I'd made the identification and gave me some coffee. He was very kind. Then some other men asked me some questions, then thanked me for coming down and told me I could go home. Which I did."

"Do you remember exactly what they asked you?"

"Whether Arthur had been on drugs—I assured them he was not. Then they asked if he might have had any knowledge of poisons or any reason to take his own life, and I told them, as I told you, that was ridiculous." He paused, momentarily pensive. "And then they asked about those other men. I had no idea why they would even mention them. It was a heart attack, after all."

I was relieved to realize that he so obviously wanted to believe his heart attack theory that the can of worms I'd nearly opened earlier had been set aside. I didn't see any real reason to contradict him.

"Did the police say who had found his body?" I asked.

Bell nodded. "The paperboy, apparently. He'd come to collect and found the front door open, just a bit, and had looked in and seen Arthur…"

"The front door was open?" I interrupted, then cursed myself mentally for having done so. But having jumped in, I figured I might as well finish it. "Was that something he did very often—leave his door ajar?"

Bell looked both surprised and thoughtful. "No. No, it isn't. Not at all. I mentioned that fact, but they didn't seem to think it significant."

Sirens were wailing somewhere in the back of my head, but they were too far away to guess what they were trying to tell me.

"Did you have a chance to go through his things?" I asked.

He nodded.

"Was anything at all missing?"

Bell shook his head. "No. I took the responsibility of disposing of all his things after the funeral. The furniture and larger articles were sold at auction, the rest sent off to his family in Ohio. I knew everything Arthur had, and it was all there." Suddenly, his brows came together, and his face took on a blank look. "Except…"

I've never taken pauses well. "Except?" I prodded.

Bell was obviously concentrating, his eyes focused on a spot somewhere in space. "Photos. There were some photos missing from his photo album. The album was in the living room, which I thought a bit strange, and as I was packing it away, I couldn't resist looking through it—for old times' sake, as it were—and there were three or four photos missing."

"How could you tell?"

"Arthur was very neat about certain things," he said. "His photo album was full—photos on every page, all neatly arranged chronologically with little captions underneath. Once, long ago, I'd commented on that, and he said he liked to hold on to his past. And yet when I looked that last time, there were two or three pages in a row with photos missing, and the captions had been removed. That was most unusual, now that I think of it."

The sirens in my head were very loud, now. "Did you happen to keep the album?"

He shook his head. "No. The family demanded they get everything that wasn't sold. Not very nice people, I'm afraid. They insisted on a complete inventory both before and after the sale, and an exact accounting of every penny."

"Do you have any idea of what the missing photos might have been?" This time, I didn't mind the pause.

Bell traced the outline of his lower lip with thumb and index finger, opening and closing the gap between them time and again. Finally, he shook his head. "No, I'm sorry. I can't. They were from the period I was back in Missouri, but that's all I can say for sure. Probably of people I did not know, anyway."

A tiny buzz—this one not in my head—signaled the opening of the shop door. Bell rose, smoothed his tie against the front of his shirt with his palm, and said: "I'm afraid I have a customer. Was there anything else you'd like to know at the moment?"

"No," I answered, also getting up. I reached into my shirt pocket for my card. "You've been very helpful, Mr. Bell," I said, handing him the card, which he slipped into his jacket pocket.

"I'm not quite sure how," Bell said, motioning for me to precede him from the alcove/office, which I did. "I'm afraid I rambled far more than I intended."

The customer, a paunchy little man in a very expensive looking jumpsuit, smiled and waved at Bell, who nodded and smiled in return. Walking with me to the door, Bell turned and offered me his hand, once again the efficient businessman.

I took it and, just before releasing my hand, his grip

tightened momentarily. "But tell me, Mr. Hardesty—what have you learned?"

Once again our eyes locked.

"Something, Mr. Bell," I said. "Something very important. I just wish I knew what it was."

CHAPTER 4

Damn it, why do I always expect things to be easier than they inevitably turn out to be? (Well, what the hell do I expect—a printed program?)

I carried on this internal bitch fight all the way downtown and to the front door of the El Cordoba Hotel. A grimy, narrow building six stories high, with a four-story, equally grimy double-faced sign—the kind they always use in cheap detective movies to illuminate otherwise-dark street-facing rooms.

The recessed entry was littered with torn newspapers, used paper cups, and the assorted dust-blown trash that adds to any downtown's charm. In one corner, near the door, a small brown paper bag was molded around an empty wine bottle. A real classy joint, the El Cordoba. It was the kind of place where the management's experience with dead guests was, you could tell, considerably higher than, say, the Waldorf's.

The lobby consisted of four overstuffed chairs and a sofa—all bolted to the linoleum tile floor; two artificial palms which had seen better days, and three large blow-up photos of the city, taken around 1947. A small glass panel in a closed fire door showed a long, murky corridor with doors set at monotonously regular intervals. An elevator, somewhere behind the door, whirred and ground noisily on its way up or down.

The "front desk" was a window with dirty glass that ended about four inches above a small ledge for registering. As I'd halfway expected, no one was in the tiny room behind the window.

A badly smudged card scotch-taped to the wall just to the left of the window and just above a small black button announced: "Ring Bell." I rang bell.

A not-unattractive guy, about 30, wearing a black form-fitting T-shirt about three sizes too small, and with more muscles than anybody has a right to have, came into the room from somewhere out of my line of sight. His massive arms, from the point they first became visible at the edge of his sleeves down to his wrists, were covered with tattoos. You name it, he had it: black leopard with bright red claw-marks; "U.S.M.C.;" "Born to Raise Hell;" the guy was a walking billboard for a tattoo parlor. I could just imagine what lay beneath the T-shirt.

"Help you?" he asked through the small circle cut from the center of the window.

"Is the manager here?" I asked.

His eyes narrowed, suspiciously. "The day manager is," he said, flexing his muscles and expanding his already awesome pecs. "You're lookin' at him. What you need?"

"Some information."

He snorted like someone who'd heard that line once or twice before. "Library's three blocks down and to the left," he said.

"Yeah, I know, but my card's expired. I'm looking for some information on one of your guests…"

"We got lots of guests," he said, impatiently.

"Yeah, well this one's dead. Died here, as a matter of fact. Room 414. Name was Bobby McDermott."

Again the muscle flexing, and I was reminded of a gorilla guarding his home territory. "You a cop?" he asked, eyes narrowed. "You're a cop, you show me your badge."

"No, I'm not a cop," I said. "I'm a private investigator."

"You a fag?"

"Unless that's an invitation, I can't see what my sex life has to do with what we're talking about."

"Bobby was a fag," he said, almost sadly. The fact that he called him "Bobby" wasn't lost on me.

"Yeah, I know. So what?" I watched his reaction, and saw him loosen up a bit.

"You don't care he was a fag?"

"Look, I wasn't paying his rent. I don't give a shit what he did in bed, or with whom." I let that sink in a minute, then said: "You know Bobby pretty well?"

He eyed me intently for a few seconds, then said, defensively: "Bobby was a good guy."

Feeling fairly confident that all the hairpins were by now pretty well dropped, I said: "Yeah, so I understand. Look, I think you and I and Bobby have a lot in common…" I let that one soak in a second, too, "…so whatever you tell me will stay in the family, so to speak. I just want to know a little more about the circumstances of Bobby's death. It might really help a lot of people."

I reached into my billfold and pulled out a ten, but when I started to push it through the slot at the bottom of the window, he waved it back and shook his head.

"Bobby was a good guy," he repeated. "We wasn't exactly pals, but I helped him out with a room a couple of times, and he…" the hulk of a manager dropped his eyes and actually blushed "…he helped me out some, too, if you know what I mean."

I knew.

"Was the room in Bobby's name that night?" I asked.

The manager shook his head. "Huh-uh. Some other guy's."

"Did he and Bobby come in together?"

"I dunno. I'm the day manager; I get off at six, six-thirty. Bobby, he come in around ten from what I hear. Night manager's on then. It was me who found Bobby next morning when I was making my morning check. I didn't even know he was in the hotel."

"Whose name was the room registered in?"

The hulk retreated to the dark recesses of his mind while his right hand scraped slowly under his nose, exposing the word "L O V E" tattooed on his knuckles. "Kane…? Kearn…? I looked it up; should remember it." He was talking to himself more than to me. A quick, unconscious flexing of every muscle in his upper torso announced his mind's return. "I'll look it up for you. Just a second."

He bent over, nearly out of sight, then straightened back up, holding a loose fistful of 3x5 cards. Tamping them straight on his side of the registration ledge, he began sorting through them with obvious efficiency.

"Kano." He said, stopping at one of the cards. "B. Kano. Baltimore, Maryland."

"Can I see it?" I asked.

He shrugged. "Sure," he said, and slid it through the slot toward me.

Other than the night manager's almost totally illegible scrawl indicating the room number (414) and the price, the only non-printed words on the standard registration form were: "B. Kano, Baltimore, Maryland," in nondescript block letters.

"Did the police ask to see this?" I asked.

"Sure. But they didn't make any big deal of it. Most of the people stay in a dump like this use fake names, anyway. 'B. Kano's got more class than 'John Smith,' though."

"Yeah," I said. But I made a mental note of the name "B. Kano" anyway, just in case.

"What time's the night manager get in?" I asked.

"'Bout six. But if you're plannin' to talk to him about this Kano guy, you can save yourself a trip."

"Why's that?"

He took the card I'd slid back to him and tapped at the night manager's scrawl. "Ernie drinks a little," he said. "He's got a real nice handwriting when he's sober, but I can tell from this shit he was blotto. And when Ernie's shitfaced, a herd of elephants could come through the door and he couldn't tell you what color they were."

"Any chance Bobby might have signed in as B. Kano?"

He shook his head. "Could be, but I don't think so. If Bobby'd wanted a room, he'd 'a set it up with me earlier. Ernie, he's married and got six kids. He don't make no freebie arrangements with guys. Besides, on freebies, nobody signs no cards."

"Did you ever consider becoming a detective?" I asked, only half joking. I was genuinely—if grudgingly—impressed by the fact that somebody apparently lived under all those muscles and tattoos.

He grinned and blushed again, but said nothing.

"I really appreciate your talking with me, uh…" I began, before remembering I didn't know his name.

"Brad," he said, still grinning.

"…Brad," I repeated.

"Sure thing," he said, giving me a half-wave, half-salute.

I returned the gesture and turned to leave.

"Hey!" Brad's voice called out, and I turned again toward

the window. "You ever need a room sometime, maybe you an' me could work somethin' out…"

"You got it," I said, allowing myself a brief flash of erotic fantasy. I gave him another smile and a wave, and left.

*   *   *

At exactly five o'clock I called Mike Sibalitch. The phone rang eight times before it was answered with a rather breathless "Hello?"

"Mr. Sibalitch. This is Dick Hardesty; we spoke this morning and you asked me to call at five."

"Oh, yeah. Sorry if I sound a little out of breath," he said, sounding a little out of breath. "I was out working in the yard, and I was halfway up the hill."

"That's okay," I said. "I was hoping you might have a few minutes to talk to me about Gene Harriman. I have to be out that way later this evening, and if you're going to be home, maybe I could stop by and talk to you first."

"Sure. I work eleven-to-seven, and I leave here about ten. What time did you have in mind?"

"Well," I said, doing some quick mental calculations of distance and travel times between Bellwether and Partridge Place, "is seven o'clock okay?"

"That'll be fine. You know how to get here?"

"I've got a city map—it shouldn't be any problem," I said.

"Fine," he acknowledged. "See you then." And he hung up.

I had just enough time to stop at the apartment to clean up a little, change my shirt (it was still in the upper 90's, and I've never found an antiperspirant that works), and grab a quick bite to eat before heading out again.

*   *   *

Sibalitch's house was a comfortable two-story colonial in an area of homes whose resemblance to a Hollywood back lot set was heightened when a kid the spitting image of Beaver

Cleaver peddled past me on his bike. Built on a hillside lot, the house sat quite a distance back from the street and slightly above it. A brick stairway and sidewalk led to the paneled front door, which was adorned by a brass lion's head knocker. Ignoring the bell, I rapped the knocker three times, pleased by the solid, no-nonsense sound.

The door opened almost immediately, and I got my first glimpse of Mike Sibalitch—tall, slim, with short black hair. His dark blue short-sleeved sport shirt and white pants accented his Slavic good looks.

"Mr. Hardesty," he said, opening the door wide, rather like a soldier shouldering arms. "Come in."

I entered the tiled foyer and he closed the door before extending his hand. His handshake was firm and dry, and even before we stopped shaking, he was guiding me into the living room.

We sat in a pair of wing-back chairs flanking the fireplace and facing one another over a glass-topped coffee table.

"Things have been a madhouse around here since Gene's death," he said, taking a pack of cigarettes from his shirt pocket and offering me one, which I refused with a 'no, thanks' head shake. "Insurance men, forms, papers; Gene's brother in for a week from Miami. A real mess."

"You seem to be taking it all very well," I observed.

Sibalitch shrugged and picked up a leaded-crystal lighter from beside a matching crystal ashtray on the coffee table. "I don't have much in the line of choices, do I?" he said.

"You and Mr. Harriman…Gene…were lovers, I gather?"

He lit his cigarette, took a long drag, then held it away from him and stared at the glowing end for a moment before releasing the smoke in a slow, deliberate stream. "For two years, seven months, and twelve days," he said. He looked up suddenly and met my eyes. "If that sounds saccharinely romantic, I can assure you it wasn't meant to be. Ours wasn't exactly a fairy-tale relationship, but it worked for us."

I nodded. "You were the one who found his body?"

"Yeah," he said with a sigh. "I came home one morning and

found him dead in bed. I thought he was sleeping, at first, but there's something about being dead that doesn't allow that illusion to last for long."

"Did the police tell you the cause of death?"

"No," he said, "I told them."

Surprised, I asked: "And that was…?"

Neither his face nor his voice betrayed the slightest emotion. "Natural causes," he said as casually and noncommittally as though he were talking about computer circuits.

"Gene had had a really serious case of rheumatic fever as a kid; it did a real number on his heart. He always said he wouldn't live to see 40."

"And what did the cops say?"

"Nothing. They must have believed me; they got into a huddle and talked among themselves for a few minutes, then they just looked around to see in anything looked suspicious, I guess. They asked me if he ever used drugs, or if he'd been depressed, stuff like that. I told them 'no'. Then the coroner came to take Gene away, and the cops left. I told them to check with Gene's doctor."

"Did you happen to see the death certificate?" I asked.

"Yeah, Gene's brother showed it to me; it gave the cause of death as 'respiratory arrest,' which is pretty generic, I suppose: you stop breathing, you're dead."

Sibalitch lit up another cigarette, then sighed. "I guess I was just lucky to have Gene as long as I did. Just wish it had been longer, but this sort of thing just happens, I suppose."

I got the impression that he, like Martin Bell, believed what he wanted to believe.

"Did the police ask you any questions you thought were a little out of the ordinary?" I asked.

Sibalitch thought for a moment. "Not really. Other than them asking if Gene or I had any access to any kind of poison. That was when I told them about Gene's heart condition. When they were talking among themselves, I heard one say something about dusting for finger-prints—why in hell they'd have to do that I have no idea, but then another one said something I couldn't hear and that was the end of it.

"The rest of the time was mostly small talk while we waited for the coroner."

"Do you remember any of it?" I asked.

"Well, you have to realize I was really struggling not to fall apart in front of a bunch of cops. I wouldn't be surprised if they knew we were gay, but they didn't ask and I wasn't about to tell them that was my lover lying there. They just asked some general stuff, whether Gene or I knew some guy named Roger, stuff like that."

"Do you mean Rogers?" I asked. "Alan Rogers?"

He looked at me even more strangely and his eyes narrowed. "How did you know his first name? Is something going on that I should know about?"

"Nothing. Nothing," I reassured him, lying through my teeth. "It's just that there have been several…ah…unusual deaths recently. Alan Rogers was one of them. I suppose they thought Gene might be another one."

Sibalitch pursed his lips for a minute, then said: "Oh, that's probably it. But he wasn't, of course."

Before he could pursue that line of thought any further, I jumped in with a question: "Did you by any chance know Alan Rogers?"

Sibalitch shook his head. "*I* didn't; it's possible Gene might have but I have no way of knowing."

Gene Harriman had been Victim #2. When they couldn't develop a positive link between Harriman and Alan Rogers, the first victim, the police apparently evolved their random-deaths theory; one which, given their lack of any real interest in a bunch of dead "*pre*-verts," would have held up quite well in the subsequent deaths.

Sibalitch ground his cigarette out in the ashtray. "Exactly what is it you're investigating, Mr. Hardesty?"

Since Sibalitch obviously wanted to believe his lover died of natural causes, I had no reason to destroy the illusion. "I have a client who is tying to locate certain people for reasons a little too complicated and boring to go into," I lied. "I had reason to believe Gene might have known some of them."

"I know most of Gene's friends," Sibalitch said. "Maybe I can help you."

"I was hoping you might," I said, truthfully this time. "Do any of these names mean anything to you: Arthur Granger… Clete Barker…Arnold Klein…Bobby McDermott?"

Sibalitch pursed his lips and wrinkled his brow in thought—reminding me briefly of Tex/Phil—and then said: "Arnold Klein. Short guy, balding, glasses?"

"I couldn't tell you, I'm afraid," I said, feeling a familiar wave of frustration. "I've never seen him."

"Well, Gene did know a guy named Arnold Klein, if it's the same one. He came to a party we gave right after we bought the house. I only met him that one time, and that's been over two years, now."

"Could you tell me anything about him?" I asked. "How well did he and Gene know one another?"

Sibalitch thought for another moment or two, then shook his head. "Sorry, I couldn't tell you. I think they were more acquaintances than real friends—if they'd been friends, I'm sure I'd have seen him more than that once, or heard more about him from Gene."

That made sense. "Do you happen to know how or where they knew each other from?"

Again the head shake. "No, I'm sorry. It was a big party and I really didn't have much time to spend with any of the guests, individually. Gene and he spoke for quite some time, though, as I recall. I only remember him at all because Gene commented after the party that he and Arnold had been through a lot together. I asked him what he meant, and he said 'Believe me, you don't want to know.' I didn't press him on it."

"Ummmmmmmm," I said, taking mental notes. "And none of the other names—Granger, Barker, McDermott—strikes any kind of chord?"

A long pause, and finally: "No. I'm afraid not."

"How long did you and Gene know each other before you became lovers?" I asked, following the ghost of a hunch.

"A little less than three months. Not a long time, but long enough."

Something was going on in the back of my mind, but I'd be damned if I knew what it was, or what it meant. I had the feeling Sibalitch had told me something, just as Martin Bell had—but what? There were just too many pieces; like doing a jigsaw puzzle without having the photo on the box to go by. I also had the strong feeling that Sibalitch could tell me a lot more, if only I knew the right questions to ask—but I didn't, and the whole thing was getting me more frustrated by the minute.

Maybe, when I knew some of the questions, I could come back and talk to Sibalitch again. I glanced at my watch. "I've taken up enough of your time, Mr. Sibalitch," I said, getting up from my chair, my motions reflected by his own. "I really appreciate your cooperation and I hope you won't mind if I call on you again if I have more specific questions."

"Not at all. I'm just sorry Gene isn't here to help you. He probably could have done a much better job than I."

We'd reached the front door and shook hands again.

"I'm really very sorry about Gene's death," I said, and meant it. "I hope you'll accept my condolences, belated as they are."

Sibalitch opened the door onto the still-hot twilight. "Thanks," he said. "Feel free to call if there's anything more I can tell you. Good night."

"Good night," I said as he closed the door.

*   *   *

It was only a little after seven thirty, so I stopped at a hot dog stand for a chili cheese dog with sauerkraut (light on the onions—you never know) and a chocolate shake.

Nothing is harder to kill than time, and it was only eight forty-five when I arrived at 27 Partridge Place, a two-story stucco neo-American Indian Pueblo affair complete with rough-hewn beams protruding at regular intervals from just below the flat roof. Lots of arches, indirect lighting, and a courtyard that went on forever—a fact the builders tried to hide with lots of plants and splashing fountains. I viewed all this though the wrought-iron security gate, but hesitated to ring the buzzer to Apartment D just yet. Instead, I took a walk around the block, mentally smoking a cigarette, and tried to sort out a few of the more promising-looking pieces of this increasingly frustrating case.

It was still only five 'til nine when I got back to Tucson Manor, or whatever it was called, but I was tired of waiting, so I pressed the buzzer and waited. And waited. Three more leanings on the buzzer produced no results. Maybe it was broken.

I decided to go to a drugstore I'd seen about three blocks away to call, and was just walking back toward the sidewalk when a yellow Porsche purred up in front of a fire plug directly in front of the building. A head, leaning over from the driver's seat, appeared in the open passenger's side window, called out: "Dick Hardesty?"

I'd only heard that voice once, on the phone, but Tim's taste in men, as usual, turned out to be excellent. "Mr. Miller?" I asked, moving toward the car and the full impact of one of the most beautiful faces I'd ever seen on a man.

The passenger door opened, and Miller said: "Get in—we'll drive to the garage." I fleetingly hoped the garage was somewhere in Yucatan. "Sorry I'm late," he said, flashing me a smile that could melt chocolate, "but the shoot ran later than I expected, and I had to stop at the store for a few things."

We shook hands as I climbed into the passenger seat, and he shifted into gear, the Porsche gliding smoothly away from the curb and almost immediately making a sharp right onto a down ramp. A wrought-iron gate whooshed noiselessly open as the car purred through, then closed with equal silence behind us. Miller whipped expertly into a narrow stall between two concrete pillars and turned off the engine.

"Need help with the groceries?" I asked, indicating the four full bags on the narrow ledge behind us.

"That'd be great," he said as we got out of the car.

In the cleaner light of the garage, Gary Miller was even more spectacular than I'd thought. His hair was either blond or prematurely gray—whichever, it was perfect for him; his eyes Mediterranean blue. About six-two, he looked like something Michelangelo might have sculpted on one of his better days. His tan made him appear to have been spray-painted café au lait, though the fine gold hairs on his arms did everything but sparkle.

In short, *'Be still, my beating heart!'*

We extricated the bags from the car and I followed him out of the garage and up a flight of stairs into the long courtyard.

Apartment D proved to be on the ground floor, and the complex a series of unconnected buildings joined by a continuous walkway at the second-floor level. It would be relatively easy to come and go on the ground level without being seen.

Once inside the apartment, Miller flicked on the lights and I followed him into the kitchen, where we deposited the grocery bags on a cobalt-blue ceramic counter. Miller rummaged quickly through the bags, took out a few things and popped them into the freezer, then said: "I can put the rest of this stuff away later. Come on into the living room and sit down."

The living room was everything Rholfing's was not. Less formal than Sibalitch's house, the key to Miller's lifestyle was apparently quiet masculinity and innate good taste. The walls were hung with paintings I'd have given an arm for—one, in particular, a nude male study in browns and beiges.

"Alan did that," Miller said, noting my interest. I didn't have to ask who the model had been. "That…" he said, indicating a portrait of a rather brooding young man as dark as Miller was light "…is Alan. I should get rid of it, but somehow just can't bring myself to do it. Alan was very talented…Can I get you a drink? Please sit."

I settled onto the chocolate brown, corduroy sofa. "A drink would be fine. Bourbon and water or bourbon and seven, if you have it."

"Sure thing," Miller said, moving to a small wet bar in the dining area just off the living room. "I'm a manhattan man, myself."

While he made the drinks and took a short side trip to the kitchen for ice, I took in the rest of the apartment still within eye range. It was the kind of place I wished *I* lived in—you know how it is; you're perfectly happy with your own place, but then you see one of those furnished model homes, and…

"If it's too weak, let me know." I looked from the full glass about a foot in front of my face up a strong, tanned hand along a beautifully muscled arm carpeted with tiny golden hairs to a biceps-hugging T-shirt across a wide expanse of chest over a wisp of chest hair curling over the collar of the shirt up a bronze-pillar neck and over a matinee-idol chin (cleft included) into a face that was just too fucking beautiful for any one human being to have. He smiled, as if at some private joke. "I have that effect on some people," he said, obviously reading my mind. But he was still smiling, and I knew he wasn't being vain—just truthful.

"Sorry," I said, blushing furiously, I'm sure.

"Hey, don't be," he said, seating himself halfway down the sofa from me. "My face, as they say, is my fortune. As far as I'm concerned, it's just a gift from my parents. But without it I'd have to get an honest job."

The silence while we sipped our drinks was broken only by the clink of ice against glass, and when I looked again at Miller, he was staring at me, no longer smiling. "Now, what about Alan?" he said.

"I'm not exactly sure," I admitted. "Actually, I'm working on a case that really doesn't involve Mr. Rogers…"

"Alan," he corrected.

"…Alan directly. But I felt he might know some people I'm trying to locate. Now that he's…uh…dead, I thought perhaps you might be able to help me. How long had you and Alan been together?"

Miller sighed deeply, took another drink from his manhattan, and laid his free arm along the back of the sofa. His fingers were disturbingly close to my own shoulder. "Only about eighteen months," he said. "Alan was my first lover; can you imagine that? I'm thirty-two years old, and Alan was my very first relationship."

I resisted the temptation to speculate as to why, and I needn't have bothered, because he went right on talking.

"This probably sounds like bullshit," he said, looking directly at me, "but it ain't easy being beautiful." He gave a quick half-smile, but his eyes were serious, and sad. "I came out when I was twenty-two and started modeling. I was married at nineteen, had two kids…hated every minute of it. So when I found out that there were other guys who liked guys, I became a number-one whore—and I could have just about anybody I set my sights on.

"So, then, about two years ago, I was sitting at home one night getting ready to go out, and I started thinking about all the guys I'd been with, and I realized I couldn't remember a single thing about any of them; they were all one big blur. I knew then that it was about time for me to settle down… Do you have a lover?" he asked.

"Nope. Not at the moment."

He nodded head as though I'd proved his point. "Then you probably know that wanting a lover and finding a lover are two different things."

We each took another sip from our drinks. I was uncomfortably aware of Miller's hand just inches away. It wasn't that I thought he was coming on to me; it was that I rather wished he were.

"So, just under two years ago I met Alan. He was bright, and talented, and charming, and I said 'Aha! This is what I've been looking for.' We courted—just like the squarest of square straight couples—I did everything but formally propose. What I didn't know and didn't find out until much later when I suddenly came down with a case of the clap after being faithfully and happily married to Alan for six months, was that monogamy wasn't part of his vocabulary. Alan was something of a male nymphomaniac—a satyr, I think they're called. If you had a dick, you qualified."

Miller drained his glass and got up from the couch in one quick motion. "Like a refill?" he asked.

"No, thanks," I said. "This one's fine."

He continued talking as he made himself another manhattan.

"You can imagine what that did to the old ego, finding out your one true love is everybody else's not-so-one, not-so-true love. Fucking egos!"

He came back into the living room and sat down beside me on the sofa, much closer this time. I was becoming very warm.

"It happens," he said, letting his arm drop into the small space between us. "But it doesn't happen to me! I've been spoiled rotten all my life just because I've got a nice-looking face and a halfway decent body."

Now there, I thought, *was the understatement of the century.*

"Do you know what?" he asked, turning to face me full-on. "When I found Alan dead—just laying there in bed like he was asleep, except Alan never slept on his back—I was sure somebody had killed him. But there was no blood, no mess, no sign of a struggle, nothing out of place. Just Alan, dead in bed. The police asked me all sorts of questions, and said they'd get back to me. They never did. When I tried to find out what was going on, no one could—or would—tell me anything. But I kept after them and finally, somebody told me—off the record—that he'd committed suicide; he'd taken some kind of poison."

"And you accepted that?"

"Yes, it wasn't really that much of a surprise, if you knew Alan."

"Had he ever threatened suicide?" I asked.

Miller sighed again, and took a sip of his drink before answering. "Only two or three times a week. Alan was a temperamental artist—aren't they all?—and a spoiled brat. Every time we had a fight, he'd threaten to kill himself, just to make me feel guilty. He was very good about laying on guilt. But we hadn't had a fight in days. I just can't figure it out. I still don't know where he got whatever it was that killed him. He didn't use drugs; I don't think there was anything in the medicine cabinet that could be considered lethal. It wasn't as though he drank a glass of Drano—I gather that's a pretty messy way to die, and Alan would never have chosen a messy way to die."

He looked at me closely. "And then you show up, asking

question. These other people you mentioned…who are they and what do they have to do with Alan, exactly?"

I took another sip of my drink before answering. "I don't know for sure that they have anything to do with him," I said, feeling pretty certain I was lying and hating myself for it. "Alan's name was just one of several, and I'm trying to find out if there is any link at all between them, and if so, what it was."

Miller set his drink on the coffee table and sat back on the sofa. "Okay," he said, "so run them past me. If Alan knew them, there's a possibility I might have, too—unless they were tricks of his. He was thoughtful enough not to rub my nose in them."

"Gene Harriman." I watched his face for any reaction. There was none.

"Nothing."

"Arthur Granger."

"Nope."

"Clete Barker."

"Sorry."

"Arnold Klein … Bobby McDermott."

He shook his head. "Not doing too well, am I?" he said, apologetically.

"Don't worry about it," I said. Alan Rogers had been the first victim; again, the police apparently hadn't gotten back to him after the other bodies were discovered.

"Any more?" he asked.

"That's it. Back to the old drawing board, I guess." I drained my glass down to the ice cubes, but when Miller pointed to it and raised an eyebrow as a question, I shook my head. "No, thanks," I said. He looked disappointed and I mentally kicked myself for passing up an opportunity to stay longer. I try never to mix business with pleasure, but I'm not a fanatic about it, and in Gary Miller's case… .

"Was there anything at all out of the ordinary about the house that day—and especially the bedroom?" I asked.

Miller shook his head. "Not a thing. The maid had been in the day before, and she always leaves the place spotless. It usually took us a couple of days to mess it up again."

"So nothing unusual?"

"Afraid not. Except for the phone number," he said offhandedly.

"What phone number was that?" I asked.

"Behind the night stand, on the floor. I dropped my keys and when I bent down to look for them, I saw it. I have no idea of how it got there unless it fell out of his wallet somehow on the day he died. It couldn't have been there the day before or the maid would have found it and picked it up. It wasn't like Alan to collect phone numbers—as I said, he tried not to rub my nose in his little adventures.

"Right after I came down with the clap, I laid down the law to him. I told him if I ever caught him tricking on me, I'd break both his arms and kick his ass out on the street. I'm sure it didn't slow him down, but it made him very discreet."

"Did you keep the phone number?"

"Yeah," he said, hoisting his well-rounded buns off the sofa to reach into his back pocket for his wallet. He thumbed through it for a minute, then came up with a folded piece of paper—a piece of bar napkin, it appeared. He handed it to me, and I opened to read: "Ed. 896-7897."

"Did you ever call it?" I asked.

He shook his head. "No. I was tempted, but what good would it do? I don't even know why I kept it. Must be my masochistic side."

I refolded the paper, having—I hoped—memorized the number, and handed it back to him.

He waved it away. "Keep it," he said, and I casually slipped it into my pocket without comment.

"Did Alan keep a photo album?" I asked.

"Not that I know of," Miller replied. "He always looked down on photographs and photographers—which I always found kind of ironic, considering my line of work; to Alan, painting was the only valid form of artistic expression."

We sat silently for a minute or so, and I was again awkwardly aware of his nearness—and that his eyes were on me.

"Well," I said, getting up quickly, "I really appreciate your help, but I've really taken up enough of your time, Mr. Miller."

"Gary," he said, getting up and taking my extended hand.

Now, there are handshakes and there are handshakes, and *this* was a handshake! I looked up and met his intense blue eyes staring into my own.

"Maybe we could get together again sometime, socially," he said, "—after Alan has gone a little farther toward the back of my mind."

"I'd like that," I said, and this time I definitely wasn't lying.

CHAPTER 5

I slept right through the alarm, which I'd deliberately set for a change, and didn't get out of bed until nearly eight-thirty. Pissed at myself though I was, a long shower and about a half-gallon of Murine put me back in fairly good shape, and by the time I'd shaved and gotten dressed, I was feeling downright chipper.

I made it to the office just before eleven, checked with my service, looked through the mail, and seriously considered buying a new air conditioner. Maybe when this case was over, I could afford one—a nice little window unit that I could take with me whenever they decided to tear down the building; an action already about thirty years overdue.

Reluctantly, I forced myself out of my dream world back into reality. Aside from possible future social benefits, my visit to Gary Miller had produced the first tangible—please, God—clue in the case: the phone number Miller had found close to Alan Rogers' body. Granted, it wasn't much, but it was all I had. I started to look for the folded paper I'd stuck in my pocket when Miller gave it to me, and cursed myself when I remembered it was still in the shirt, which was hanging on the bedroom doorknob at home. *Stu-pid, Hardesty! Stu-pid!*

Ed. That much I remembered. But the number…was it -7897? Or -7987? Yeah: -7897. (I hoped.) Chances were that nobody would be home, but I had to give it a shot. I picked up the phone and dialed.

On the second ring there was the familiar click of an answering machine and a voice, warm and masculine, said: "Hello; this is Ed Grayley." Bingo! "I'm not able to make it to the phone right now, but if you'll leave your name and number at the tone, I'll get back to you as soon as possible." A three-second silence was followed by a mellow chime rather than the usual irritating metallic beep.

"My name is Dick Hardesty, Mr. Grayley. I'm a private investigator and I hope you might be able to give me some information on a case I'm working on. It won't take but a minute of your time, so if you could call me at 555-8274 I'd appreciate it. Thanks."

So much for that. I returned a couple of calls left with my service, made an appointment for a haircut, and then decided to go down to Hughie's on the off chance of running into Tessie, the guy Bud, the bartender, had told me might know some more about McDermott.

Actually I rather hoped I might find Tex/Phil there. (We Scorpios are great people except for an annoying tendency to be ruled by the crotch.)

Hughie's at one in the afternoon is very much like Hughie's at any other time of day—dark and clammy as ever, a few unfamiliar shapes sprinkled around, but basically the same people sitting on the same stools drinking the same drinks. Bud was at the far end of the bar under the comparative glare (maybe 40 watts) of a new beer sign, deep in conversation with a short number wearing what I vaguely made out to be a beard and a billed army cap. Tex/Phil was nowhere to be seen.

I stood at my usual spot about a third of the way down the bar, waiting for my eyes to become accustomed to the gloom. It was nearly two minutes before the guy Bud was talking to noticed me and, with a jerk of his head, signaled my presence to Bud. Bud turned, waved and, still talking, reached into the cooler for a frosted glass and drew me a dark.

"How's it going, Dick?" he asked, making an elaborate flourish of taking a napkin off a stack and placing it in front of me.

"Okay, I guess," I said as he set the glass down on the napkin, little rivulets of melted ice immediately forming a wet circle around it. I fished into my billfold and pulled out a bill.

"You ever talk to Tessie?" he asked.

"No…I never made it back after the last time I saw you."

"Well, you're in luck," he said. "Tessie came in early today." He turned his head and called down the bar: "Hey, Tessie! Guy here to see you."

The bearded number with the army cap picked up his drink and came toward us.

"That's Tessie?" I asked.

"That's Tessie. Used to be one of the hottest drags in the city. He's going through a butch period right now." Tessie set his drink down beside mine as Bud made the introductions. "Tessie, this is Dick."

"I think I'm in love," Tessie said with a winning smile, and his handshake was solid. "What can I do for you, Dick?"

"I understand you knew Bobby McDermott."

Tessie apparently missed the past tense. "Sure, I know Bobby," he said. "Haven't seen him in a while, though."

"And you're not likely to, I'm afraid," I said. "Bobby's dead."

"You're shitting me!" Tessie looked genuinely shocked. "What happened?"

"An accident," I lied.

"Jeez, that's a shame. Bobby was a nice guy—fucked up, but nice. And, honey, that cock of his…" Tessie spoke the last with a reverence that left little doubt as to how well he had known McDermott.

"Did you know any of the people he hung out with?" I asked.

Tessie shook his head. "Not really. Bobby was sort of a loner. He had a lover who makes me look like King Kong—a real bitch, that one. Bobby used to drop by my place for a little consolation whenever he could get away, and I understand he hustled some but, you know, I can't remember his ever mentioning anybody by name. Isn't that strange? But Bobby was always more action than talk, if you know what I mean."

"I have a vivid imagination," I said. "Do any of these names mean anything to you, then? Alan Rogers; Gene Harriman; Arnold Klein; Clete Barker; Arthur Granger?"

"Huh-uh," Tessie said, shaking his head. "Not that I know of. I might recognize them if I saw them, but the names don't mean anything. Sorry."

I shrugged. "That's okay. When's the last time you saw Bobby?"

Tessie thought for a minute. "Oh, God, it must be about three weeks or more. No, I take that back…or do I? No, three weeks is about right. He came by my place." There was a moment of reflexive silence, then, not a little wistfully: "I sure am going to miss that stud."

The ringing of the phone was barely audible over the jukebox throb and Bud, who'd been washing glasses at the sink almost directly in front of us but apparently tuned out to our conversation, moved off to answer it.

"Tessie!" he called; "It's for you." He clamped his big hand over the mouthpiece. "And tell your fucking tricks this ain't your fucking answering service."

Tessie sighed dramatically, then gave me a wink and a smile. "Ah, the price of fame," he said, and headed toward the wall phone just outside the men's room at the far end of the bar. Bud waited until Tessie picked up the phone, then hung his receiver back on the hook.

I finished my beer and ordered another.

"Tessie any help?" Bud asked as he set the beer on a new napkin.

"Not much, I'm afraid," I said.

"Sorry about that," Bud replied.

I drank my beer slowly, sort of waiting for Tessie to get off the phone—not that I had anything in particular to talk to him about, but simply as a matter of politeness. But when, after ten minutes, Tessie was still leaning against the wall, the phone under one ear while he examined his fingernails in the dim light, I finished my second beer. Leaving some change on the bar for Bud, I caught Tessie's eye and waved goodbye. Tessie smiled, blew me a kiss, and went back to examining his fingernails.

I debated on whether to return to the office or just go straight home and have the service forward Grayley's call—assuming he'd call at all—but decided I really should go by the office even though it was probably hot enough in there by now to bake bread.

I was right about the temperature in the office, so I stayed only long enough to call the service and tell them to give Grayley my home number if he called, and that I'd be home in fifteen minutes.

*   *   *

The early edition of the evening news had just come on the tube when the phone rang.

"Dick Hardesty," I said, picking up the phone.

"Mr. Hardesty." I recognized the voice from the answering machine. "This is Ed Grayley; I just got home and got your message." In the background I could hear the sound of a TV tuned to the same channel I had on.

"I appreciate your promptness," I said.

"I work for an airline," he said. "After a while, it gets so that promptness isn't so much a virtue as it is a way of life."

As with Gary Miller, there was something about Grayley's voice I instinctively liked. It wasn't a bedroom voice, like Miller's, but it produced good vibes nonetheless.

"What can I do to help you, Mr. Hardesty? I'm very big on intrigue."

I laughed. "Sorry to disappoint you. It's nothing very glamorous, I'm afraid. I just wanted to ask you a few questions about Alan Rogers."

There was a pause, then: "I'm sorry? What was the name?"

"Alan Rogers."

"Damn; now I'm disappointed. I was all set to help you solve some exotic case with my brilliant deductive reasoning, but I'm afraid I don't know any Alan Rogers."

"That's strange," I said. "He had your phone number."

"He did? Did he say where he'd gotten it?"

"I'm afraid not. He's dead."

There was another pause. "Oh. I'm sorry to hear that. But then I'm right—there is some deep, dark mystery. A murder?"

"I...uh...I don't know that that's exactly accurate," I said, knowing full well that I thought it was exactly accurate. "But I am curious as to how he got your phone number."

"I tell you what," Grayley said, his voice as familiar as if we'd known each other for years. "Are you doing anything right now?"

"Just talking to you," I said.

"Good. I do hope you don't think me presumptuous, Mr. Hardesty, but mysteries really do intrigue me, and the fact that it's none of my business doesn't get in the way of wanting to know more about this one—and to find out how this Rogers guy got my number. Would you like to meet me for a drink and we could talk about it?"

He *was* being a little presumptuous, but what the hell? His voice set off some pleasant flashes of erotic fantasy, and…

"Sure," I said. "Where do you suggest?"

"What part of town are you in?" he asked.

"I'm in the Bradford area."

"Great! Do you know where the Carnival is?" I did; it was about five blocks away from my apartment. A nice, comfortable, gay businessmen's bar with a good if slightly expensive restaurant.

"Yeah," I said. "I know where it is."

"How about meeting me there about six-thirty? We can catch the tail-end of their happy hour."

"Fine," I said. "I hope they don't mind shorts—I'll be wearing white shorts and a white T-shirt with blue trim."

"In this weather, shorts are the uniform of the day," Grayley said with a laugh. "I'll get into an old pair of cutoffs with a white tank top. Don't worry; we'll find each other."

Somehow, I was sure we would.

"Okay," I said. "See you at six thirty."

As I hung up, I wondered why in hell I was suddenly feeling like a teenager going to his first prom?

*   *   *

I'd always liked the Carnival, but I didn't get out to the bars all that often, and there were at least six within a mile radius of my apartment. It attracted a nice mix of average gays and lesbians, and your average heterosexual wandering into the place probably wouldn't immediately catch on to the fact that it was a gay bar.

On this hot afternoon, summer business suits predominated, since most of the clientele had stopped in directly from work. I was, thank God, the only one in white shorts and a white T-shirt and, as usual, I was about ten minutes early.

I took a seat near the door where I could watch everything and everyone in the mirrors behind the bar and ordered an Old Fashioned.

At exactly six thirty, a pair of cutoffs and a white tank top walked into the bar, filled out by a six-foot, naturally muscular frame. Dark brown hair, cut short, dark eyes, a nice tan, and a definitely interesting face. Not Gary Miller, but decidedly handsome. And sexy. No doubt about it; my kind of guy.

He saw me, smiled, and walked over. "Made it," he said, extending his hand. We shook hands and I was favorably impressed by the casual firmness of his grip.

"Do people set their watches by you?" I asked, smiling, as he pulled out the stool beside me and sat down.

He grinned. "I know," he said. "Sometimes I think my punctuality is a curse. But it drives me up a wall to be late."

He motioned for the bartender and ordered a whiskey sour.

"I'm the same way," I said while we waited for his drink, "only I always manage to be too damned early."

Grayley paid for his drink, and I noticed that his hair, which I'd first seen as dark brown, was actually black, beginning to turn salt-and-pepper. It only added to his appeal.

"So tell me, he said, rushing directly to business..." he grinned, "...more about this Rogers thing."

I fished into the small pocket in my shorts and pulled out the folded piece of napkin, handing it to him. He unfolded it, looked at the note, and raised his eyebrows.

"Yep. That's my writing, all right. Let me think. Since it's handwritten, it apparently wasn't business-related. And I don't give out my home number casually—which hopefully speaks well for my lack of promiscuity."

I sipped my drink while he thought aloud. "Alan Rogers. Alan Rogers. Alan. Hmmmmmm." Suddenly, his face brightened. "Yeah! Sure! Now I remember. This was a guy I met at the Cochise Club, oh, hell, it must be nearly two months ago, now. Nice guy, I thought at first. We danced a couple of times and he came on pretty strong. He asked me for my number and

I gave it to him, but when I asked for his, he said he couldn't give it to me because his lover was too jealous. Well, that took the wind out of my sails real fast. If I'd known he had a lover I never would have given him my number. Maybe I'm square, but I don't believe in playing that kind of game, and I told him so. And that was about it."

"A gentleman of principal, I see," I said.

"I try," Grayley said. Noticing that my drink was nearly empty, he signaled for the bartender with his free hand.

"You never saw him again?" I asked.

"Huh-uh. Like I said, I don't see any percentage in going to bed with someone who has a lover. Too strong a middle-class, middle-west upbringing, I guess. I learned a long time ago that if someone will dump a lover for you, I know damn well one day he'll dump you for someone else."

"Two minds with but a single thought," I said.

He raised his glass: "I'll drink to that."

"Can you tell me anything else about him?" I asked, as we set our drinks back on the bar.

"Like what?" he asked. "What are you looking for?"

I felt like saying 'That's two different questions,' but thought better of it and shook my head in frustration. "I wish to hell I knew. I'm open for anything…" I caught his quick smile, "…no pun intended. Was he there with anyone?"

Grayley shook his head. "Not that I saw. The place was jammed wall to wall as usual, but I didn't see him talking to anyone else."

"Did he say anything about his life; about people he knew; anything?"

Grayley took another drink. "Other than that he had a lover? Hmmmmm. Don't forget, this was only one night—or, rather, a small part of one night—a couple of months ago. The only reason I remember him at all is because he was very attractive, and as I told you, I don't give out my phone number to that many people. That's no bullshit, by the way."

I was somehow flattered that it seemed important to him that I believe him.

"But let me think," he continued, then paused to run one hand over his chin. "No, honestly, I don't remember him saying all that much of interest. Said he was an artist…I remember that because I hoped for a minute he was going to ask me up to see his etchings. But other than that, no personal information. Just the usual bar chatter. And some pretty strong hints at the kinds of beautiful music we could make together. I, I gather, was to be the bassoon and he the oboe."

We both laughed.

The bartender finally came over and we ordered another round.

"I'm really sorry I couldn't be more help to you," Grayley said, and I got the distinctly pleasant feeling he meant it. "Can you tell me anything about what you're working on, or is that some sort of privileged information?"

"Well," I said, trying to be both truthful and tactfully evasive at the same time, "it started out pretty simple, and the further I get into it, the more complex it seems to be getting. I'm not quite sure what's going on, myself. Which is a pretty frustrating feeling, I can tell you."

Grayley grinned. "Yeah, I've been frustrated once or twice myself."

Our drinks arrived, and Grayley insisted on paying.

"I always sort of fantasized about being a detective," he said as the bartender rang up the sale. "When I was a kid, it was a toss-up between being Sam Spade and a fireman. So I ended up with the airlines."

"What do you do for them?" I asked, genuinely curious.

"I'm what's known as a Passenger Service Representative for Pan World. Sort of a social director for VIPs traveling with us—make sure they're happy while waiting for their flights, keep the madding crowds at bay, that sort of thing."

"This is your home base, then?"

"More or less. I work all over, actually. I spent the last year in Nairobi, Kenya; before that it was Singapore; Guam; Anchorage; Lima. Frankly," he said, giving me another grin, "I think I'd rather be a detective."

I shook my head. "Any time you want to switch jobs, just give me a call."

"I think I might like that," he said, and I couldn't tell if he was kidding or not.

"Look," I said on an impulse, "if you're not heading off for Pago Pago or someplace equally exotic tonight, how'd you like to have dinner with me? The food's pretty good here, and maybe you could give me a vicarious tour of Nairobi."

He gave me a smile that was definitely not teasing. "I think I might like that," he said.

Something told me I might, too.

I was right.

CHAPTER 6

Remember the last time you had an evening when just about everything went right? When you really enjoyed just being with someone, relaxed? Well, that was my evening with Ed Grayley. We hit it off as through we'd been pals since grade school. He was quick, funny, totally unaffected and, best of all, he really seemed to be having as good a time as I was.

If I'd met Ed while out cruising, I'd have jumped on him in a minute, but I had to remind myself that this wasn't really a cruising situation. And while I was sure I was getting some definite vibes from him, I knew this wasn't the time to start letting my crotch rule my head. I had a strong suspicion we were going to see each other again and, as I told myself, good things are worth waiting for.

Was he a potential suspect? I hoped not, but at this point who wasn't? The fact of the matter was that this was the first time I'd had a chance to get my mind off the case, and I took it. Selfish of me, maybe, but... .

It was ten-forty-five when we left the Carnival. Ed had an early-morning flight of foreign dignitaries he had to look after, but said he'd give me a call late in the afternoon; there was a movie playing locally that we'd talked about and both wanted to see.

The crackle of lightning and a blast of thunder that sounded like it originated next to my bed jolted me awake at three a.m. The rain came down in buckets, and I thought about my open office window. Then I figured: "Fuck it; at least it'll be cooler tomorrow," and went back to sleep.

*　*　*

The rain had ended by morning, and with it the heat wave. I got to my office around nine, halfway expecting to open my door to a tidal wave of water from the open window. But somebody up there must like me, because there was only a small puddle under the window ledge—apparently the wind must have been blowing in the right direction, or the rain had fallen straight down. There was, however, a new dark, wet spot on my ceiling directly above, indicating that the office over mine had shared the same experience.

At nine thirty, the phone rang.

"Hardesty Investigations," I answered in my best professional voice.

"Hi, there, sailor—new in town?" It was Tim.

"As a matter of fact, I am," I said. "Know where a guy can go for a little action?"

"Well, I'm not home right now, but…"

"Okay, Charlie Tuna, what's on your mind?"

"Not much," he said. "I'm on my coffee break and thought I'd see how things were going with you."

I leaned back in my chair and gazed out the window at nothing in particular. "Kind of slow," I said. "But I'm more sure than ever that there's a link between all six guys—that it isn't just some sicko wandering around with a cyanide-filled amyl bottle picking up casual tricks. Mind you, I haven't got a single thing to go on other than my hunches and a few very weak leads, but I'll be willing to bet a bundle I'm right. Anything new on your end?"

Tim laughed. "You want to rephrase that?"

"Bright little rascal, aren't you? You know what I mean."

"Yes, I know. And no, nothing's new here. Just your usual garden-variety corpses—car accidents, stabbings, shootings—the everyday stuff. It's been nearly two weeks since our unknown friend pulled a number. Maybe he ran out of cyanide."

"Let's hope so," I said. "But even if he has, it won't be much help for the six guys he's already knocked over."

"True," Tim agreed. "You manage to talk to everyone on that list I gave you—excluding the corpses, of course?"

"Just about. I'm debating on whether or not to even try with Klein's parents. I will try the roommates, though."

"Good luck," he said. "So what did you think of Gary Miller?"

"You were, as always, right. He's quite a guy."

"The voice of experience?" Tim asked.

I ignored him. "I haven't gotten in touch with Bill Elers, either, but I'll try to drop by his place today and leave a note for him to call me."

"I'll keep my fingers crossed for you," Tim said, sincerely. "Well, look, I'd best get back to work. Keep me posted, huh?"

"You bet—you're still my Number One Son, don't forget. 'Bye. And thanks."

"Ciao," he said, and hung up.

No sooner had I replaced the receiver in its cradle when the phone rang again, startling me. I waited until the second ring, then picked it up again.

"Hardesty Investigations."

"Mr. Hardesty!" It took only five syllables for me to recognize Rholfing's twitter.

"Yes, Mr. Rholfing," I said, again using my all-business voice. "What can I do for you?" *Shit! I did it again!*

But Rholfing apparently wasn't into 'cute' this morning. Instead, his voice was breathless with excitement. "I know, Mr. Hardesty! I know!" He sounded like a ten-year-old with a secret he was just dying to share.

"I'm glad, Mr. Rholfing. What is it you know?"

He was nearly panting. "I know those people you were asking me about! I remember them all!"

I felt the adrenaline pumping through me, but tried to keep my voice—and myself—calm. "Are you sure?" I asked, hoping this wasn't just another of his ploys to get me into the bedroom.

The excitement in his voice was tinged with just a slight pout. "Of *course* I'm sure. I was so stupid not to have known the minute you mentioned them, but as I told you, I'm absolutely dreadful with names. But I remember other things. Alan Roberts or Rogers or whichever it is is a painter; Clete Baker is a big man with a football player's body and the IQ of a baked potato. Arthur…uh, what was it…*Granger* has this thing for truck drivers and Hells Angels rejects—I think he and Clete had something going there for awhile, but I'm not sure; and Arnold…uh…Klein may look like a mouse, but he's a certified sex maniac, I can tell you. Am I right? Am I?"

I hoped he was near the bathroom, because it sounded as though he might pee in his pants any second. But by this time, I was getting nearly as excited as he was. Still, I fought to keep my voice cool.

"It sounds like you've got it just about right," I said. "But how do you know them? What's the link between them, if any?"

"Oh, there's a link, all right. But that's all part of the surprise! I've got to tell you in person. Why don't you stop by tonight around five thirty? We can have cocktails, and I can tell you all about it."

I wanted to reach through the phone and grab him by the neck, but I kept my voice calm. "Well, couldn't you tell me now…"

His voice changed from excited schoolgirl to Gestapo interrogator. "*No, I can't!* You probably know already, anyway. You haven't kept me up to date as you promised, Mr. Hardesty. I mean, I hardly know what's going on… ."

"I'm sorry, Mr. Rholfing," I said, trying to soothe him and feeling only slightly guilty. "I'll tell you what; why don't I just come by now, and we can talk about it?" I could always bring along a cattle prod in case he got too out of hand.

"I'm afraid I'm going to be…uh…*busy* this morning, Mr. Hardesty," he said, his voice, like a fluid transmission, shifting from scorned bitch to coy suitor once again. "Five thirty would be much better. I should be…*through*…by then."…a girlish giggle. "Oh, yes, and I have some more money for you. And you *will* tell me everything you've been doing on the case, won't you?"

"Yes, of course, Mr. Rholfing. I don't mean to press you, but perhaps if you could give me some clue over the phone, I'd be able to do something on it today and have something more for you by this evening." *Tell me, you twit!*

"Well, maybe just a little clue won't hurt. As I say, you probably already know, but…" There was a muted sound of bells in the background. Rholfing's voice regained its excited tone. "Oh, dear, I'm sorry, but my gentleman caller has arrived. I must go. See you at five thirty. Ta-taaa." And with that, he hung up.

I held the receiver to my ear for a full five seconds before finally hanging up. A quick knotting in the pit of my stomach told me something was wrong. Very wrong. Oh, God, what was it? I felt like I'd eaten a cannon ball. My mind raced through the file cabinets of my memory, frantically searching for…something.

Oh, shit! ShitShitShit! I fumbled frantically through my address book, looking for Rholfing's number. Finding it at last, I dialed, cursing the phone company for the slowness of its equipment. An eternity passed, and finally…a busy signal! A fucking busy signal!

I literally ran out of the office, mentally fighting with myself to keep from panicking.

I made it to Rholfing's apartment as fast as I could. Every inch of the way, my mind kept repeating: *Alan Rogers, Gene Harriman, Arthur Granger, Clete Barker, Arnold Klein. Let me be wrong about Rholfing's 'gentleman caller'! Let it not be who I think it is!*

Rogers, Harriman, Granger, Barker, and Klein: Rholfing didn't know they were dead!

*   *   *

The door to Rholfing's apartment was unlocked. I knocked several times, then entered cautiously, my stomach still in knots. "Mr. Rholfing?" I called, knowing full well there would be no response. The phone, on the bookshelf near the bedroom hallway, was off the hook.

Rholfing was lying on the bedroom floor, in a flowered kimono. The bed itself had been obviously made, then turned down. There wasn't a wrinkle on it.

I bent over Rholfing's body to see if there was a pulse and detected the very slightest scent of almonds. His eyes were open and his face, though the muscles were now relaxed, suggested that he had died with a look of surprise.

His lips and fingernails were distinctly blue and he was, of course, quite dead, although his body was still warm. Getting up quickly from the body, I looked around the room. Nothing appeared to be out of place.

Using a handkerchief to open drawers and doors, I went through his dresser and closets. I really didn't know what I was looking for, but they always do that sort of thing in detective stories, and I figured it couldn't hurt. On top of a built-in chest of drawers in his walk-in closet was Rholfing's wallet. I opened it and found five one-hundred-dollar bills, four twenties, six tens, several five's, and some singles.

The $500 was, apparently, what Rholfing had intended to give me that night and, feeling guilty as all hell but rationalizing that Rholfing intended me to have it—and that the case was not over yet—I took the five bills, leaving the rest in the wallet.

A check around the rest of the apartment revealed nothing, and there was little point in my hanging around. Using my handkerchief, I replaced the phone on the cradle, waited a moment, then picked it up again. When I heard the dial tone, I called the police, saying there had been a death and giving Rholfing's address and apartment number. Then, leaving the front door slightly ajar, I left.

*   *   *

Regardless of what you may have read, heard, or seen, finding dead bodies is not a regular part of a private investigator's life—at least, it sure as hell wasn't a part of mine. In fact, the last dead body I had seen was five years before at my uncle's funeral. I do not count corpses as one of my favorite things.

After leaving Rholfing's—taking the stairway instead of the elevator and hopefully without being seen—I went straight home and took a long, long shower.

Unlike a lot of people, I don't sing in the shower. I think. And God knows I had enough to think about. Seven men were dead—one of whom, if I were to choose to wallow in mental masochism, which I didn't, might not be dead now if I'd bothered to let him in on what little I knew. If only I'd told him at the outset that the men I asked about were dead! Still, no matter how I rationalized it, I had a strong sense of guilt.

Rholfing had said he knew the other victims—all of them. But how? What was the link? What did they all have in common? Why didn't anyone I'd talked to know any of the other victims if, indeed, the victims had known one another? Mike Sibalitch had said he'd met Klein, and that Harriman and Klein had known one another, but that could well be coincidence. Even in a city this big, the gay community is relatively small, and that any two gay men might know each other couldn't be described as unusual.

Most frustrating of all, of course, was the question of whether the chain ended with Rholfing, and if not, just how long a chain was it?

There was something. Something in the back of my mind that wouldn't identify itself. Something each of the men I'd talked to had told me that might be what I needed. Damn! It was right there—why couldn't I grab hold of it?

I'd learned years ago that my mind could be a real rotten sonofabitch. Whenever I pushed it too hard, it would deliberately keep just out of my reach. I had to calm down; to force myself not to think too hard. It would come, tiptoeing up behind me when I wasn't looking, whispering the answer in my ear.

Unfortunately, patience was never one of my greater virtues.

Sighing, I turned off the water, reached for a towel, and began drying myself off. I'd just finished one leg when the phone rang. Hastily drying the other, I dripped my way to the phone.

"Dick Hardesty," I said, probably sounding as though I weren't quite sure myself. The voice on the other end picked up my spirits immediately, though I didn't have the time to wonder why it should. "Dick, hi. This is Ed. I took a chance that you might be home. How are things going?"

"Ed," I said with total conviction, "you don't want to know. It has not been one of my better days."

"Hey, I'm sorry to hear that," he said, and I could sense that he was. "Anything you feel like talking about?"

"Not right now, I'm afraid. Maybe later." I forced myself to brighten up. "How come you're calling so early? Not that I mind, of course. As a matter of fact, I'm delighted you did. I needed to hear a friendly voice."

"Good. I'm glad. No special reason; I just finished work early and thought I'd try to reach you. Still feel like going to the show tonight?"

I didn't, but also didn't relish the idea of letting my sense of guilt and frustration take me too far down the path to depression. I'd been down it often enough before to know it went nowhere. "Sure," I forced myself to say, still drying myself with my free hand. "I could use a little distraction right about now. What time, and where?"

"Well, I thought we might grab something to eat first, if you'd like. I can fix something for us at my place, if that's okay with you, then we can leave from here."

"Sounds great." The thing was, despite how lousy I felt, it did sound great. *Watch it, Hardesty,* I told myself. "All I need to know is where, what time, and what I can bring."

"The where's easy enough: 481 Kenmore, number 34. I think the movie starts around eight, so would six be too early?"

"Six is fine."

"And as to what you can bring, nothing. Just come as you are."

I looked down at myself and grinned. "481 Kenmore, number 34. See you at six. But don't be surprised if I'm early."

"Whenever. 'Bye."

As I hung up the phone, I was shaking my head, a new set of thoughts crowding out the others. Why in hell was I acting like a teenage kid with a crush on his gym teacher? *You need to get laid, Hardesty,* I told myself. I'm not the kind of guy who falls 'in love' every fifteen minutes; as a matter of fact, I'd made it a rule to avoid long term entanglements. But who said this had to be a long-term anything? Relax, for crissakes! You just met the guy, and with all the pressures you're under right now, you're just a little off guard. Relax and enjoy it. Don't make a big thing out of it.

Okay, I'd convinced myself. For the moment, at least. But something told me I wasn't really fooling myself. I knew full well that the more I thought about Ed, the more I thought about Ed.

I threw the towel into the clothes hamper and started to get dressed. I felt I really should call Tim and let him know about Rholfing, but I didn't want to risk calling him at work. I decided to try him at home, later.

*   *   *

At exactly five-forty-nine I was ringing the bell on number 34, 481 Kenmore. What I'd seen of the place thus far had favorably impressed me. An older building, solid, the kind with wood beams and real fireplaces; the kind other people always live in but you can never find for yourself when you have to move.

Ed opened the door, smiling. "Ah, not a moment too soon," he said, extending his hand. We shook hands, and he closed the door behind me.

The living room was to the left of the small entry. Sure enough, there was a fireplace; peg-and-groove floors; sparsely furnished in a mixture of styles, but the overall effect was warm and comfortable.

"I just got this place when I got back from overseas," Ed said by way of explanation. "I still need a lot of things. Before I left the country I sold most of my stuff; the bulk of this has been in storage most of its life. But now that it looks like I'll be operating out of the home office for the foreseeable future, I can start doing a few things I've been holding off on."

He smiled and put a hand on my arm, casually. "What would you like to drink? I don't think I can make an Old Fashioned, but I've got just about everything else."

"Bourbon and seven or bourbon and water's fine," I said.

"Good. Why don't you come into the kitchen with me while I monkey around with dinner. It won't take long."

The kitchen, off the small dining room, was roomy and pleasantly cluttered—not messy, and a lot neater than mine, but lived in.

Ed fixed the drinks and I sat at the kitchen table while he moved back and forth between the sink, refrigerator, and stove with professional casualness.

"I hope you don't mind meat loaf," he said, pausing to take a drink from his bourbon and seven. "That, steak, and chili I can handle. Everything else is a disaster. My general rule of thumb for cooking is: if you smell it burning, it's done."

We small-talked our way through his preparations, then adjourned to the living room.

"Feeling any better?" Ed asked, handing me a coaster. "You really sounded pretty down when I talked with you earlier."

"Yeah," I said, sensing the back burner of my mind switching on despite my efforts to keep it off—at least for tonight. "Like I said, it was a rough day. I sort of lost a client."

Still, the ingredients were beginning to drop into the pot: McDermott; B. Kano; missing photos; open doors. *Later, damn it! Let me just relax tonight, okay?*

"Hmmmmm," Ed said. "Sorry about that. But a guy like you should have lots of clients."

"Yeah, usually. Mostly piddling stuff. This one's different. A lot different." I leaned forward, idly stirring the ice cubes around in my drink with an index finger. I suddenly remembered Tim. I'd tried to get him before I left the apartment, but he wasn't home yet. I wouldn't exactly feel right about asking to use Ed's phone: talking about finding corpses wasn't exactly conducive to the flow of a pleasant evening. Besides, I didn't want to bring Ed into the whole mess. I decided that if I couldn't call Tim tonight, I'd try him first thing in the morning.

Rogers: cheating on a lover; McDermott's a 'tramp'; Granger into rough types; Klein and Harriman knew each other—of course they did: Rholfing knew them all, so the odds were pretty good they all knew one another.

"Well, " I heard Ed saying, "I don't want to butt into your business, but any time you feel like talking to someone about it, I'm a good listener."

I smiled, suddenly aware of just how much I'd been wandering. Looking directly at him, I said: "I appreciate that,

Ed. Really. And I hope you don't mind if I seem a little preoccupied every now and then. I don't mean to be, but I can't seem to help it."

Ed returned the smile. "No sweat," he said.

We small-talked some more, finished our drinks, and Ed went into the kitchen to get us refills and check on dinner.

Why wouldn't Bell, Sibalitch, or Miller have known any of the other victims? What link was there in the fact that they didn't? There was one. That bastard part of my mind knew and it wouldn't tell me.

"A-hem."

Startled, I looked up to find Ed standing in front of me, holding a fresh drink. Embarrassed, I took it. "Some company I am," I muttered.

"I told you, no sweat," Ed said. "I get that way myself, from time to time."

Time! I nearly dropped my glass. "Time!" I said aloud, producing a look of surprise and slight bewilderment on Ed's face.

"Time for what?"

"Time! It's a link!" I heard myself say. I lost track of everything around me in the rush of thoughts, like air rushing into a vacuum: I wasn't even aware that I was talking aloud. "Martin Bell was out of the city for an extended period about three years ago; Mike Sibalitch had only been with Gene Harriman a little less than three years— Klein and Harriman had known each other before that! Rholfing and McDermott had been together about a year, but had known each other quite a while before that. Gary Miller and Alan Rogers had been together less than two years. Whatever they had in common has to go back at least three years!"

Ed just stood there, looking at me and shaking his head. "Whew!" he said. "You lost me way back there. Right about when you shouted 'Time!'"

I felt like a complete fool. "Oh, shit, Ed! I'm sorry. I really am! You must think I'm some sort of nut—and you're probably right."

Ed smiled and motioned me toward the dining room. "Forget it, Sam Spade," he said. "You can help me set the table. It's just about time to eat."

Time was a link!

But to what?

I got up to set the table.

CHAPTER 7

Rholfing was dead and I was, technically, without a client. But I had some of his retainer money in the bank and another $500 stashed at home. I also had a burning sensation in my gut that told me I was going to follow the case no matter how long it took or where it might lead. I still couldn't shake the feeling of responsibility I had for Rholfing's death. If he knew the victims, he knew the killer—I was positive of that much. And if I'd told him Rogers, Klein, Harriman, Granger, and Barker were dead, he would never have invited his killer in. And if wishes were wings, elephants could fly.

At seven thirty the next morning, I was on the phone.

"Good morning." Tim's voice as a bit groggy.

"Tim. Hi. Sorry if I woke you, but I've got some news I wanted to prepare you for."

"I've got VD."

"No…"

"You've got VD."

"No, damn it! We've got another death. Rholfing; McDermott's lover."

"Holy shit! That must have been the one they were wheeling in just as I was leaving. He was in a body bag, but it wasn't all the way zipped up and I thought that bleached blond hair looked familiar." He paused, then said: "But how did you find out?"

"I found him yesterday afternoon. I called the police from Rholfing's apartment, but didn't identify myself and wasn't about to stick around for them to get there. I didn't want to call you at work, and wasn't able to call after you got home."

"I had a date right after work," Tim said. "I didn't get home until late." Another pause. "I don't suppose I have to ask how Rhol…Rholfing, was it?…died?"

"Not if the slight scent of almonds and blue skin gives you any clue."

Tim gave a long, slow sigh. "Here we go again."

"Look, Tim," I said, "I really hate to put you out on a limb like this, but could you make an extra effort to find out what's going on with the police? Surely they're not just going to sit on their hands with seven deaths, and counting."

"Dream on, good sir." Tim's voice showed his bitterness. "From everything I know, they've done nothing *but* sit on their hands so far. 'Proceeding with all deliberate speed,' I believe they call it. They're positive it's a serial killer, though, which gives their lack of action a certain credibility, in their eyes at least. All they can do is wait for the next body and hope the killer makes some sort of traceable mistake." There was yet another slight pause, then: "Tell you what. I know one of our people on the force. I don't know whether he's aware of what's going on or not—I told you that rabidly homophobic police chief of ours is trying to keep this a very private party—but I'll check with him without giving too much away. It's a toss-up as to whether he'll have anything or not, but it's worth a try."

"Tim," I said honestly, "I don't know what I'd do without you! I really owe you."

"How about a partial payoff with lunch today? Maybe by that time I'll have rustled up something."

"You're on. When and where?"

"Well, I only get an hour, and I still have to be pretty careful. Can't go anyplace gay during working hours, and straight places make me nervous. Why don't you grab some fried chicken or something and meet me at the fountain in Warman Park? About noon, or a few minutes after."

"I'll be there," I said.

"Okay. I'd better get started pulling the old bod together for work. The way I feel this morning, it's going to be a major project. See you at noon."

I hung up the phone and poured myself a second cup of coffee. It was going to be a long morning.

*   *   *

I'd tried to reach Arnold Klein's number before I left the apartment, but there was no answer, so I tried again when I got to the office. Still no luck. I decided to try once more that evening, and if there was still no response from the roommates, to just drop by their apartment and leave a note for them to call me.

Which is what I also decided to try with Bill Elers, Clete Barker's lover/roommate, since neither was listed in the phone book.

I putzed around the office until the bank opened, deposited Rholfing's posthumous $500, and headed for 4427 West Avondale—Elers' apartment. I didn't really expect to find anyone home, and didn't. But I slipped my card under his door with a note asking him to please call me that evening, giving both my office and home numbers.

By the time I made it back downtown, stopped at a fast-food place for some chicken and a couple large Cokes, it was nearly noon. Warman Park is about two blocks from the City Building, where Tim worked, and I sat on the edge of the fountain—the upwind side, to avoid windblown spray—and waited for Tim.

Fortunately, Warman Park has some very nice scenery—hunky office workers, up-and-coming young execs, a few scantily-clad joggers—so the time passed quickly. Still, it was nearly quarter after when Tim showed up.

"Sorry I'm late," he said, plopping himself down on the ledge beside me. "We did the autopsy this morning on you-know-who. God, even dead he looks like a faggot."

"Any surprises?" I asked.

Tim looked at me, one eyebrow cocked. "You expected surprises?" he asked.

The breeze made a sudden shift, and a few drops of spay from the fountain began to fall around us. I grabbed the chicken and Cokes and we moved off to a shady area under a tree about twenty yards from the fountain and ten from the nearest pathway.

Tim rummaged through the sack like a bear at a campground. "God, I'm hungry!" he said. I never could figure out how someone could carve up dead bodies all day and still be hungry, but, then …

"So did you find out anything from your cop buddy?" I asked, waiting while Tim ravaged a drumstick before answering.

"Ummmmm," he said, grabbing a napkin and wiping his mouth. "Word's pretty well out in the department," he said, reaching for a Coke and a straw. He inserted the straw expertly into the slit on the plastic lid (I always end up stabbing furiously at it, usually smashing the straw beyond repair, sloshing Coke all over myself, or both in the process) and took a long drink, his eyes closed in mock ecstasy. "But it hasn't provoked much interest," he went on, finally.

"I checked with my contact on the force, and he was pretty close-mouthed. He's aware that something is going on, but apparently doesn't know any of the specifics. What he'd heard is that there's another serial killer out there, but that since he's specializing in faggots, it's not that big a thing. Now, if straights start dying... .

"I overheard the Medical Examiner—I know damn well he knows my scene, and he's pretty sympathetic to us—talking to some plainclothesman I assume is in charge of whatever investigation there might be."

Tim reached into the sack for a breast, which he attacked with the same enthusiasm he'd shown the drumstick. "Anyway," he continued between bites, "the M.E. was asking the cop how the investigation was going and it was plain as shit the cop was bored by the whole thing. No leads, no clues, absolutely no connection between any of the victims ...and get this," Tim jabbed the air with the half-eaten breast, emphasizing his point, "...his reaction to the fact that McDermott and Rholfing were 'roommates' was: 'Well, it just goes to prove these fucking faggots never learn!'"

Tim stared at me in wide-eyed disbelief. "Can you imagine that? Jesus Christ, I wanted to give that asshole an autopsy right on the spot! Even the M.E. couldn't let that one pass."

Tim finished the breast, dropped the bones onto a napkin with remains of the drumstick, and licked his fingers. "You're not eating?" he asked, as I stabbed furiously at the small slit in my Coke lid with the straw.

"Not hungry right now," I said, giving up and tearing the lid off the cup.

Tim shrugged and reached into the sack for more chicken. "Anyway, the M.E. looks at the cop and says, very calmly, 'These are human beings we're talking about.' I nearly applauded. The asshole turns about three shades of purple and says, all blustery, 'Well, of course they're human beings. We don't show any bias in our investigations. But you know how hard it is in these *home-o-sex-yool* cases; they're all so promiscuous.' He left a few minutes later, and if I never see him again, it'll be too soon." Tim paused and looked reflexive. "I'll take that back. On an autopsy table, maybe…" and he attacked his third piece of chicken.

We—I broke down and had the remaining drum stick—finished our lunch in relative silence, and it was only when we were putting all the bones, napkins, and empty cups back into the sack that Tim looked at me casually out of the corner of his eye and said: "So, you keeping anything from your Number One Son?"

Embarrassed, I blurted out everything I knew, including my certainty that whatever linked the victims lay about three years or more in the past, and my guilt over Rholfing's death. I didn't mention having met Ed Grayley, though—not that Tim would have been jealous…I just didn't want to risk the possibility.

"Come on, Dick," Tim said after I'd finished. "You can't honestly feel responsible for Rholfing. Hell, you had no way of knowing." He thought a minute, then shook his head. "But it sure is one hell of a mystery. I can almost see now what the cops are up against, even if they were convinced the deaths weren't just random. Three years is a long time, especially in the gay world. There could have been any number of links—the same bar, the same organization, or work…no, not work, I don't think; they all did different things, as I recall." He reached out and put his hand on my shoulder. "You've really got your work cut out for you," he said.

He was, as usual, so right.

After dumping the garbage in a trash receptacle, I walked Tim part-way back to his office, and he promised to call me if he learned anything at all new. I left him at the corner a block from the City Building and watched as he crossed the street. Safely across, he turned, gave me a wave, and disappeared into the crowd.

* * *

Time. *Time*. What was it Martin Bell had said about his friend Arthur Granger? Something about three years ago. Yeah, that fit. Definitely. But what had he said? 'Then, about three years ago, he went through some sort of trauma—he never would discuss it… .'

I looked up Bell, Book & Candle and dialed the number. I recognized Bell's voice even before he identified himself. "Bell, Book & Candle. Martin Bell speaking; may I help you?"

"Mr. Bell. This is Dick Hardesty calling. Do you have a moment to talk?"

There was only a brief hesitation, then: "Yes. Yes, of course. What can I do for you, Mr. Hardesty?"

"When we spoke, you mentioned that Mr. Granger had had some sort of traumatic experience about three years ago which he would never discuss with you. Do you have any way of knowing what that might have been?"

There was another moment's pause. "No. No, I'm afraid I don't, Mr. Hardesty. Arthur was really a very private person in many ways, and as close as we were, I had learned long ago never to intrude upon that privacy. He told me only what he wanted to tell me."

"Did you ever surmise what it might have been?" I asked.

"No, I did not. I only know that Arthur was badly shaken by it. If I were to speculate, I would assume it had something to do with his sex life. I believe I told you that Arthur's tastes were somewhat …bizarre."

I had a feeling Bell wasn't going to be able to open many new doors, but I pushed on. "What can you tell me about Mr. Granger's life around that time? Did he mention anything specific about his activities? His friends? Places he frequented? Anything you found unusual or out of the ordinary?"

"Mr. Hardesty," Bell said, and I could almost see his beagle face breaking into a wry grin, "Arthur's *life* was unusual and out of the ordinary. He was a brilliant man—a CPA by profession—but his personal life was chaos. As to friends, he had very few, I'm afraid. He preferred the anonymity of one-night stands and back-room bars. Nothing in his letters struck me as unusual...for Arthur."

Strike two. "Did he belong to any organizations? Any social groups? Go to any particular bar?"

The smile was still in Bell's voice. "To Arthur, variety was exciting. I never knew him to take a sustained interest in anything other than sex. And because he respected my opinion of his sexual tastes, he spared me the details of his many encounters. He...oh, I'm sorry, Mr. Hardesty, a customer has just come in. You'll have to excuse me."

"Of course, Mr. Bell," I said, feeling the familiar flat line of frustration. "I've taken up enough of your time. Thank you for talking with me. Good-bye."

Sighing, I hung up the phone.

Even though he and Alan Rogers had been together only a comparatively short time, there was an outside chance Gary Miller might know something about Rogers' past. I dialed his number, not really expecting to find him home. Luck was with me.

"Good afternoon. Gary Miller here."

"Gary. Hi. This is Dick Hardesty."

His voice was as warm and sexy as ever. "Dick; good to hear from you." That man's voice could melt the polar caps.

"I wanted to call to thank you for your hospitality the other night. I really enjoyed talking with you."

"The pleasure was mine," he said, and I could just see the East Coast being submerged in 200 feet of water. "I'd always wanted to meet a real, live detective."

"Flattery will get you anywhere," I said. "But while we're on the subject of detecting, there were a couple of questions I didn't get to ask you while I was there."

"I'd really like to ask you over to talk about it, but I'm afraid it will have to wait until I get back."

"Back?"

"Yeah. My agent got me a sportswear contract I'd been praying for. It came through late yesterday afternoon. I'm catching a plane for St. Croix in about three hours. I'll be gone a week—maybe two if I'm lucky, but the minute I get back, I'll give you a call."

"I'll look forward to it," I said, and meant it. "But before you go, could you just answer a few quick questions now, over the phone?"

"Sure; I've got a few minutes."

Keep your fingers crossed, Hardesty. "How much of Alan's past life did you know? I'm referring specifically to about three to four years ago."

"Hmmmmm…" I waited while he thought for a long moment. "Not much, I'm afraid," he said, finally. "Alan, it seems, was a congenital liar in addition to his other charms, though I was too dumb to know it until it was too late. He gave me a lot of lines, but I doubt now very many of them were true. Whatever he told me, I believed…at the time."

Shit! Another dead end! "Did he say anything you can remember about the period not too long before you met—say about a year before? Anything about his friends, where he might have hung out, any groups or clubs or organizations he belonged to? Particularly any trouble he may have been in, or any incident he was reluctant to talk about?"

"Not that I can re…oh, yes! One time, when we first met, he gave me a long story about how he'd been involved in something dark and sinister, and he was sure someone was out to get him. But he didn't elaborate. Alan was pretty vague on specifics. I believed him when he first told me—thought it was kind of exciting, in a way—but I wouldn't give you a dime for the story now."

"This story," I prodded, feeling a surge of excitement, "…what do you remember about it?"

"Not much, I'm afraid. I've been working pretty hard to erase Alan from my head. Unfortunately, it's not that easy. It's…"

His voice broke off and there was a sharp pause. Then: "Dick, you aren't suggesting there was any truth to that story, do you? Do you think Alan's death might actually...that he didn't...just die? But why? How? Why wouldn't the police have told me..."

"Hold on, Gary," I said, interrupting and trying to calm him down. "I'm not suggesting anything. I just want to know more about that story, if you can remember it."

I clutched the receiver, waiting.

Gary's words came slowly, at first, in little fragments of sentences as he tried to remember. "Alan...had gotten ...mixed up with...or hung around with, I forget how he put it...a bunch of unsavory characters, and they'd all gotten drunk one night and did something really serious...I got the strong impression from the way he told it that it was tangled up with organized crime, if you can believe that...and that the guy they'd done this thing to, whatever it was, was going to come looking for them to get even. Something like that. Does it make any sense to you?"

"Not much," I said, only half-truthfully.

"Well, as I said, Alan and the truth weren't exactly close friends. You don't think it had anything to do with his death, then, do you, Dick?"

"With a story like that, it's really hard to say," I lied. "But the guy had an imagination."

"Yeah."

"Well, look, Gary, I'd better let you get back to packing. Be sure to give me a call when you get back, okay?"

"You can count on it."

I held onto the receiver until I heard the dial tone, engaging in a little constructive fantasy, then hung up.

Okay, back to business. I didn't know whether to put any stock in that story of Alan's. From what I knew of the victims, none of them would have qualified for a "Mr. Wonderful" award, but I couldn't imagine their being involved with one another on any but the most casual of levels. And organized crime? Rholfing in a fedora and a pin-striped suit? That was stretching it beyond almost anyone's belief. Still, there was something in it that rang true; and going along with Granger's "traumatic experience," there might be a skeleton of fact among all that fantasy.

But I still found it hard to imagine those seven men, from the very little I knew about them, even having enough in common to put them in a situation that would endanger—endanger, hell: *take*—all of their lives. Damn!

I waited until about four o'clock to call Mike Sibalitch, assuming he'd be up by then, but there was no answer. I decided to go home and call him from there. Which, being a man of my word, is exactly what I did.

*　　*　　*

When Sibalitch didn't answer my five o'clock call, I felt a quick stab of panic. Supposing this case was a lot broader than I'd imagined? Supposing our cyanide friend was moving outside the select circle of Rholfing and his somehow-cohorts? Or perhaps Sibalitch was part of it! Jesus! Anyone was game! Sibalitch, Bell, Gary Miller, Bill Elers…Tim…me! *Calm down, for crissake!*

I went into the kitchen and poured myself a stiff drink. Then, on a whim that I somehow knew was more than a whim, I dialed Ed Grayley—hoping he wouldn't think I was coming on too strong; I'd talked to him every day since we'd met, and I'd just seen him the night before. Maybe I should cool it for a couple of days. Maybe. And though I tried to ignore it, I was increasingly aware that my thoughts about Ed were beginning to involve more than just my head; my crotch was having some ideas of its own.

"Hello?"

Well, I couldn't hang up now. "Hi, Ed. This is Dick. I don't mean to make a pest of myself, but…"

His laugh interrupted me. "Hey, what pest? I was just sitting here wondering whether I should pester you."

"No shit?" I asked, little-boy delighted.

"No shit. What's up?"

I sighed, then immediately hoped he hadn't noticed.

"Nothing, really. It's just been another one of those days. To paraphrase Alice, this whole thing's just getting curiouser and curiouser—and I'm getting frustrateder and frustrateder."

"Well, would you like a shoulder to cry on?"

"Yeah," I said, catching myself somewhat by surprise. "Yeah, that'd be nice."

"Okay. It's your turn to name time and place."

I thought for all of a tenth of a second. "You want to come by here? I've got a couple of steaks in the freezer—I can thaw them out pretty fast in the microwave. That, and a salad, if you don't mind something simple."

"Fine with me. What time?"

"Would ten minutes be too soon? No; just kidding. But as soon as you want's fine."

"How about an hour?"

"Great," I said, glancing at the clock on the kitchen wall. "I'll see you then." Before I hung up I remembered to give him my address, then made a quick scan of the apartment. Not exactly ready for the photographers from House Beautiful, but who cares? Domesticity has never been one of my high points.

I did put the dirty dishes in the washer and turned it on, wiped off the kitchen counter, and straightened the magazines on the coffee table. That was the extent of my cleaning. Ed didn't strike me as the kind of guy who'd mind a little dust, anyway.

I took the steaks out of the freezer and thawed them in the microwave, scrounged through the refrigerator to see what was available for the salad—finding, in the process, things I hadn't seen in months—and checked the liquor and mix supply. As a concession to the importance of the occasion, I did haul out the ice bucket and fill it with ice from the freezer.

When the doorbell rang, I didn't even have to look at my watch.

"On time?" Ed asked as I opened the door.

"Need you ask?" I said, showing him in.

"Ummmmm," he said, looking around. "Nice place."

"'Lived in,' I think they call it," I said. "I'd give you the guided tour, but you can see just about everything from where you're standing. Kitchen there, hallway there, bedroom and bath down there in the gloom somewhere. 'It ain't much, but I call it home.'"

Ed grinned. "Like I said: nice place."

"Bourbon and seven, manhattan, or something else?" I asked. "Gin? Vodka? Rum and coke? Beer?"

"Bourbon and seven's fine."

I fixed the drinks, put them on the coffee table, and gestured for Ed to sit while I went to the stereo and fiddled with the FM dial. "Any preferences in music?" I asked.

"At the risk of being kicked out the door, how about some light classical?"

"Mr. Grayley, suh, you are indeed a man after my own heart," I said, and meant it. "I'd have put on disco if you'd asked for it, but you probably wouldn't have heard much of it over the gritting of my teeth." I found the station I was looking for, and Tchaikovsky's 'Francesca di Rimini' filled the room.

"So," Ed said as I joined him on the couch, "anything in particular you want to talk about?"

I took a long swig from my drink. "Not really. It's still this damned case I'm on. I just got a little paranoid today, that's all. Paranoia isn't exactly an asset in the detective business. But what the hell, I wasn't really serious about asking you over to cry on your shoulder. Well, not totally, anyway. I don't want you to have to listen to me rant and rave about my problems."

Ed smiled. "Well, first of all, I sort of asked myself over, if you'll remember, and secondly, my job is listening to people rant and rave. At least you're not demanding to know what happened to your luggage, or why your poodle can't sit on your lap during the flight."

It was my turn to smile. "Point," I said. "But because it is your job, I don't want you to have to spend your off hours doing it. So why not tell me a little more about you, for a change. We didn't really have much time to talk last night."

Ed leaned back on the couch, took a deep breath and exhaled it through pursed lips. "There's not all that much to tell, really. We covered the basics the other night, I think. Born in

Vancouver, moved to the States when I was two; parents divorced—dad moved back to Canada, mom's in Tampa; one sister ten years younger than I, married and living in Detroit. College, four years in the Navy. Been with Pan World for…let's see…fourteen years, now. That's about it."

"Any long-term relationships?" I asked, then immediately bit my tongue. What the hell business was it of mine?

"Once," Ed said. "A long time ago. How about you?"

"Once, for five years, right after I got out of college," I said, wishing I'd never brought the subject up. "Nothing you could really consider a 'meaningful relationship' since then. I guess I've just never found anybody I could hit it off with both in bed and out. Or maybe I'm just too set in my ways. I try not to lose any sleep over it. Maybe some day…" *Diarrhea of the mouth, Hardesty*!

Fortunately, the phone saved the day, and I excused myself to answer it.

"Dick Hardesty," I said.

"Mr. Hardesty, my name is Ron Pierce. I'm a friend of Bill Elers. Bill's out of town until next week on vacation. I found your note when I came over to water his plants, and thought I'd call to let you know why you hadn't heard from him."

"Thanks, Mr. Pierce," I said. "Do you know of any way I can get in touch with him? It's rather important."

"No, I don't think there's any way to reach him. He's backpacking in the Sierras with some friends. Would you like for me to give him your number, just in case he calls?"

"Please," I said. "And thanks for calling. 'Bye."

For the remainder of the evening, Ed and I stuck to noncommittal subjects. Dinner was relaxed and enjoyable—I didn't burn the steaks, for once. We both got a little mellow with the drinks and the music and just relaxing. Before I realized it, it was midnight.

"Jeez," I said, noting the time, "I hope you don't have an early call tomorrow."

Ed shook his head. "Nope. As a matter of fact, I've got the day off. But maybe I'd better go and let you get to bed."

"I'm in no rush," I said, sorry, now that I knew he had the day off, that I'd even mentioned the time. "How about a little more Strega and coffee?"

"Not for me, thanks," he said, stretching. I was afraid he was getting ready to leave, but he made no move to get up. "I'm curious," he said.

"About what?" I asked.

"About something you said earlier."

I wracked my brain for clues and came up with none. "What was that?"

"About your never having found anybody you could get along with both in bed and out."

"Yeah?" I said, hoping I knew what was going to come next.

"Well, we seem to hit it off pretty well out of bed. I was wondering if you'd care to explore the other possibility."

I got up from the couch and extended my hand to him. "Why don't we step into my private office and discuss it?" Suddenly, I had a chilling thought. "You don't happen to have any amyl with you, do you?"

Ed shook his head. "I never use the stuff. Sorry."

"Believe me, I'm not," I said. Still holding his hand, I led him down the not-so-gloom of the hallway…

CHAPTER 8

Don't ask me where the next week went—I couldn't tell you. Mike Sibalitch, when I finally reached him, could add nothing to what I already knew. I'd remembered his earlier comment about Gene Harriman and Arnold Klein's having "gone through a lot together," which I now saw as a highly probable tie-in to whatever linked the victims, but Sibalitch was unable to elaborate on it or to give me any other pertinent information on Harriman's past.

Arnold Klein's two roommates were lovers, I found out when I eventually reached them by phone. They'd only moved into Klein's two-bedroom apartment six months before, straight from Kansas City—he'd run an ad in the paper for roommates. They could tell me nothing about him or his past. A phone call to Klein's parents, whom I tracked down through Tim, produced only sobs from his mother and a blustery interruption and hang up from his father.

I made another trip to Bill Elers' place, leaving another note to ask him to call me the minute he got back. I fervently hoped he'd be able to give me some fresh information. Without it, I was pretty well stymied.

Tim kept me posted almost daily on whatever he could find out about the police investigation, which was apparently at a complete standstill, no new bodies having come to light (thank God!), and Ed Grayley kept me from going totally bananas.

I was getting just a little concerned about my reaction—or, probably, overreaction—to Ed. I've always been a closet romantic, but I haven't been through the starry-eyed, puppy-love stage since I'd met my former lover two days after I graduated from college. That had lasted five years, but ever since we'd broken up, I'd gone out of my way to avoid getting serious about anyone. Now along comes Ed and suddenly I'm Little Mr. Wide-Eyes. And, of course, the fact that our sex together was undoubtedly the best—and wildest—I could ever remember. I'd never been with anybody—not even Chris, my ex—with whom each of us seemed to know exactly what the other one wanted or needed at any given moment. Totally exhausting, of course, but fun!

A large part of it, I recognized, was due to the frustrations I felt over this case—Ed was my escape from the pressure. Thinking about him and being with him took my mind off the fact that I was getting nowhere with the case—even though I felt deep in my gut that I was close to the answers, which made me even more frustrated.

But I didn't know quite how to handle the feeling that Ed's reactions seemed very closely to parallel my own. He genuinely seemed to enjoy being with me as much as I did being with him, and I wasn't used to that. But I had the feeling that Ed was pretty well aware of what I was going through, and going out of his way to let me work these things out for myself.

We both deliberately avoided any discussion of our past relationships since that night at my place. I was curious about his lover and what had happened to break them up, but I sensed it was a very private thing for Ed, and I knew if he wanted to tell me about it, he'd get around to it on his own. As for my relationship with my ex, Chris, well…I'd let Ed bring it up if he wanted to.

By the same token, I'd never discussed the case in detail with him—why, I'm not sure, other than that I wanted a part of my life that was all mine and apart from my work. That Ed might be a suspect himself was something I'd never seriously considered and, as I grew to know and like him, was increasingly unthinkable. Still, just out of curiosity, I'd have to ask him about the other six victims.

* * *

I was mentally rehashing the case for the twelve-thousandth time, sitting at my desk in the office, when the phone rang. I took the pencil I'd been pretending was a cigarette out of my mouth and picked up the receiver.

"Hardesty Investigations."

"Is Dick Hardesty in?" I didn't recognize the voice.

"You've got him," I said.

"This is Bill Elers. I just got back into town and got your messages. What was it you wanted to talk to me about?"

Elers! Finally! "Actually, Mr. Elers, it's about Clete Barker. I was very sorry to hear of his death, but I'm working on a case on which my client feels Mr. Barker may have had some very important information. Since you and he were…close…I believe you might be able to help me."

"Well, I…"

Sensing the hesitation in his voice, I tried to head him off at the pass. "It would only take a few minutes, Mr. Elers, and it's really very important. Unfortunately, it's a little awkward trying to go into it over the phone. Could we meet and discuss it in person? I'd really appreciate it."

There was a pause, then: "Yeah. Sure. Why not? When did you have in mind?"

Whew! "Would right away be convenient? Like I say, it will only take a few minutes."

Another moment's hesitation. "Okay. I guess so. I'm just unpacking…"

"Don't worry about it," I interrupted. "I'll try not to get in your way. I'll see you in about half an hour. And thanks."

I hung up before he had a chance to change his mind.

*   *   *

"Door's open," Eler's voice called out in response to my knock. I turned the knob and went in. "I'm back here, in the bedroom," the voice said. The apartment's layout was quite a bit like mine, so I had no trouble finding my way.

Elers was standing by an open closet, placing a sleeping bag on a high shelf. He was dressed only in cutoffs, and my first impression was: 'if his front is half as imposing as his back, he must be some specimen!' When he turned around to face me, after closing the closet doors, I saw I was right. He had the kind of body most guys only dream of, outside of porno flicks—not a ten-hours-a-day-at-the-gym body, but a natural, athletic build with everything in just the right proportion and in just the right place.

"Hi," he said, without smiling but in a pleasant-enough tone.

"Hi," I replied, watching as he moved to the bed and began sorting through a large pile of clothes.

"I hope you'll excuse me," he said, pulling various-colored socks out of the pile like a magician pulling rabbits out of a hat, then tossing them into a smaller pile by themselves at one end of the bed, "but this is the first chance I've had to do laundry in a couple of weeks, and I start work again tomorrow. You wanna sit?" he asked, nodding toward a chair in one corner of the room.

"No, thanks. I'll stand," I said.

He went back to sorting through the clothes. "So what did you want to know about Clete?"

"There were some people he knew—maybe you might know them, too." I mentally crossed my fingers, then did a quick review of the three victims who'd died before Barker. "Did the police by any chance ask if you or Mr. Barker knew an Alan Rogers, a Gene Harriman, or an Arthur Granger?"

Elers stopped his sock-sorting in mid motion and looked at me. "Yeah. Yeah, they did. How did you know that?"

"Well," I said, beginning my now-familiar lie, "it seems the police are working on a related case that involves some of the same people."

"No way," Elers said, his defenses going up. "Clete never had so much as a parking ticket."

"I'm not implying that he was involved in anything," I said, using what was becoming my standard reassurance line. "I just have reason to believe he may have known them. Did he?"

Elers stared at me for another moment or two, then went back to his sorting, apparently appeased. "I never heard of any of them," he said. "If Clete did, it must have been a long time ago."

"There were a couple of other names," I said.

Elers didn't even look up this time. "Go ahead," he said.

"Arnold Klein, Bobby McDermott…"

Elers looked up, briefly. "Yeah. I know Bobby McDermott.

I was sort of seeing him when I first met Clete. That was a long time ago; I haven't seen Bobby in years." He returned to his laundry.

Bingo! I felt just a tad giddy. "How about..." Jesus, I had to think of his first name...I don't think I ever used it! My mind flashed to the driver's license I'd seen in his wallet. Kyle Bernard Rholfing. Kyle! "...Kyle Rholfing?"

Elers looked up again. "Bleached-blond nelly queen? Real pain in the ass?" I nodded. "Yeah, I know him too. Not very well, though, and I'd just as soon keep it that way."

I didn't tell him there was little chance of their ever becoming better acquainted now. I was surprised to find my mouth was dry. "How did you know Rholfing?" I managed to ask, hoping he couldn't hear my heart pounding.

Elers turned to put several pair of folded shorts into the bureau behind him. "I think he lived on those fucking stairs," he said, over his shoulder. "Every time I'd go over to see Bobby, there Kyle'd be either going up or coming down the stairs. He tried to put the make on me so many times I finally took to walking up the back way just to avoid him. That's how I met Clete, as a matter of fact. He was coming down the stairs one day while I was going up. He was probably trying to avoid Kyle, too."

Fireworks went off in my head. "McDermott, Rholfing, and Barker all lived in the same building!" I said, to myself but aloud.

"Yeah," Elers said, looking at me as if I weren't quite bright.

Of course! Rholfing had said that! (*'Bobby and I lived in the same building.'*) And he said something else...what in hell was it? It didn't register at the time... *'there was this absolutely terrible affair in the building....'* Why in *hell* hadn't I made that connection before? Maybe that was what my brain and gut had been trying to tell me all those times!

"And Gene Harriman, Arnold Klein, Alan Rogers, and Arthur Granger lived there, too!" I was still talking more to myself than to Elers, but he had no way of knowing that, so it's no wonder he probably thought I was a little strange.

"I couldn't say," Elers responded, still looking at me as he put a shirt on a hanger. "I didn't go there all that often, and I never met anybody else who lived there."

"Something happened in that building just about the same time," I said, directing myself to Elers this time. "Did you know anything about it? Did either Bobby or Clete... or Kyle, for that matter...say anything to you about it?"

Elers looked puzzled. "No, not that I know of. What happened?"

"I don't know," I admitted. "That's what I'm trying to find out. It was pretty serious, I gather. Are you sure Clete never mentioned it in all the time you two were together?"

Elers hung up the last of his shirts and began sorting through the socks again, looking for mates. "Huh-uh. Never."

Now it was my turn to look puzzled. "Strange," I said.

Elers gave a small shrug without looking up from the pile of socks. "Not so," he said. "Like I told you, Clete wasn't much on talking."

"But then Bobby or Rhol...Kyle..." I began, but Elers cut me off.

"See, like I said, I met Clete while I was seeing Bobby. Actually, Bobby and me were just fucking buddies, and when I started hanging around with Clete, he wanted me to stop seeing Bobby. I told him okay, but Bobby and me kept getting together now and then on the side. Well, then I got the clap from Bobby and gave it to Clete and the shit really hit the fan. I stopped seeing Bobby for good, then, and Clete told me to go fuck myself. We didn't see each other for nearly five months, and when we finally got together for good, we agreed we'd never even mention the past. And we didn't. Whatever you're talking about must have happened in those months when I lost track of Bobby and Clete. I haven't seen Kyle since. He's probably still haunting stairways."

If only you knew! I thought. "Where was the building?" I asked. "Do you know the address?"

Gathering up the paired socks—three mismatched singles still laid on the bed—Elers put them into a bureau drawer. "Can't remember the address, exactly," he said. "But it's on

Hutchins, near Elk. You can't miss it—it's narrow, four stories, looks like an old New York brownstone." He picked up the mismatched socks, inspecting them as if he were looking for clues as to the whereabouts of their mates. Then, with a shrug, he tossed them into the open drawer with the rest of the socks and closed it.

Gesturing for me to follow, he led the way into the living room and motioned me to a chair. I sat down, and he sat on the edge of the couch, leaning forward, elbows on knees, hands folded.

"What else can I tell you?" he asked.

"I was just curious," I said, hoping I wasn't opening a can of worms, "how Clete died, exactly. What did the police say?"

Elers sighed and stared at his hands. "They didn't, in so many words, but I gather they suspected a drug overdose."

"Was he into drugs?" I asked.

Elers stared at the floor a moment before answering. "I thought he was done with that shit," he said. "He'd had a problem with it before we got together, I knew, but I would have sworn he was clean since we got together. I don't know why in the hell he'd go back to it; everything was going pretty well between us, and I can't imagine he'd deliberately fuck it up by doing something so stupid. I was so goddamn mad at him for killing himself like that—I guess I still am."

"I'm sorry if I'm treading on sensitive ground," I said.

With a half-smile, Elers brought his eyes back in my general direction. "No, that's okay," he said. "It's probably good to talk about it. I guess I've been trying too hard to forget. That's how come I went on this camping trip—to get away, sort of. Well, now I'm back and I've got to get on with my life."

"You'll do okay," I said. I sensed it was time for me to leave, and I got up from the chair.

"One more thing before I go," I said. "Is there anything more you can tell me about the building or the people who lived there?"

Apparently relieved to be off the subject of his lover's death, Elers leaned back on the couch and thought for a moment. "Not much," he said, finally. "You know the area—it's a gay ghetto. Clete's building was all gay, of course. It's small for the neighborhood —sort of sandwiched in between two bigger buildings. A real nice place. I'm sure I must have at least seen some of the other guys who lived there—I vaguely recall a couple—but I never officially met any of them. Probably wouldn't recognize them if I were to see them again."

I refrained from telling him it was very unlikely he would ever see seven of the building's tenants again.

"How many apartments were in the building—any idea?" I asked.

"Like I said, it's a small building. There were only two apartments on the floor Clete lived on, so I imagine there'd be a total of eight."

Eight apartments, seven deaths! The jigsaw puzzle was suddenly turning into a picture. "Look," I said, "I don't mean to push on this thing, but it's really very important. Can you remember anything else at all about the building or the guys who lived there?" I had an out-of-left-field thought. "Does the name 'B. Kano' mean anything at all to you?"

Elers ran his hand under his chin, as if checking his beard. "God," he said, "it's been a long time. Kano, you say? Kano…Kano…that does ring a bell, somehow. Let me think a second…"

I waited; Elers thought, his fingers moving back and forth across his chin. Suddenly, his eyes brightened. "Yeah! There was this real good-looking kid lived in one of the ground floor apartments. He had this little toy poodle about the size of a dime—real cute little thing, if you like poodles—it used to sit in the window all the time. His name was Kano."

"The kid's?" I asked.

"No, the poodle. The dog's name was 'Big Kano.'" The kid was out walking him one day when I was coming in and I asked what the dog's name was and he said it was 'Big Kano.' I remember because here's this Munchkin dog with a name you'd expect on a Great Dane."

The pieces were falling into place almost audibly. "What

else do you remember about the kid?" I asked, hoping my excitement wasn't showing.

Elers shook his head. "Not much. He was a real beauty, like I said, but real shy. Always friendly and polite, but he never volunteered any information."

"Did he live alone?" I asked.

"I don't know; I never saw him with anyone. On the one hand, I can't imagine him not having guys crawling all over him, but on the other, he was so damned shy…"

"Can you describe him?"

Eler's eyes wandered off, following his thoughts. "Let's see …about five-ten, slender, medium-brown hair; mid-20s, I'd say. Sexy—you know…he didn't flaunt it; I don't think he even knew it. Oh, yeah…and ice blue eyes. You don't see many brown-haired guys with eyes like that."

Okay, that ruled out Arnold Klein—Sibalitch had described him as being short and dark. Alan Rogers' self portrait didn't match the description. McDermott, Rholfing, and Barker were automatically out, since Elers knew them. That left Arthur Granger and Sibalitch's lover Gene Harriman. Granger was 40, and even if the years had been especially kind, from what Martin Bell had told me I couldn't picture him being the guy Elers described. Still, you never know. I'd have to check it out with Bell or Sibalitch—or better yet, with Tim, who'd seen all the bodies.

"Hello?" Elers' voice jolted me back to reality, and I realized I must have just been standing there staring off into space. I gave Elers an embarrassed grin.

"Sorry about that," I said. "Guess I got a little distracted."

"No problem," Elers said.

"I know it's tough for you, but could you tell me just how and where you found Clete's body? It was you who found him, wasn't it?"

Elers stared at me for a moment without speaking. Then: "Yeah, I found him. He was in the bathroom, apparently just ready to get into the shower…the water was running." He gave a little snort and shook his head. "Funny," he said, "Clete always dug sex in the shower. Ironic he should die there."

I felt a twinge in the pit of my stomach that could not be described as "funny."

"I don't suppose you found anything near the body to indicate what he'd taken—no syringes, needles, anything like that."

Elers shook his head. "No. How did you know that?"

"Just a guess."

"He must have got it somewhere outside and then came home to clean up."

"Did Clete keep a photo album?" I asked, not wanting to get Elers to thinking too much about the obvious flaws in that scenario.

Elers' face registered his surprise. "Hey, that's wild!" he said. "Why did you ask that?"

"Just curious," I lied again. "Why?"

"Clete didn't have an album," Elers said. "He kept a bunch of photos in an old shoe box. He must have been going through them just before he went in to shower, because the box was sitting on the bed…"

"Do you know if he had any pictures taken while he lived in that building?"

Elers gave a quick, palms-up gesture with his hands. "I dunno; he might have. You want me to look?"

"Would you?" My gut told me that if Barker had had any photos from that period, they wouldn't be in the box now. But …

Elers got up and went back into the bedroom. He returned a moment later with a shoe box and motioned me into the kitchen. "Let's look at 'em in here," he said. "We can use the table."

Primitive cultures believe that photographs capture the soul; I've always considered them to be what William Blake called "spots of time"—the tiniest fragments of a life, suspended for as long as the photo exists. Spread on the table in front of us were fragments of Cletus Barker's life—people and things and places long gone or altered or changed, now, but still parts of him.

Some of the fragments Elers was able to identify; most of them he could not. There were, as I expected, no photos of the period, the place, or the people who most concerned me.

Elers had picked up a photo of the two of them in happier times, and was staring at it, his face sad. "I just wish I'd been here," he said. "Maybe I could have done something…"

"I doubt it," I said sincerely. "It would have happened anyway, I'm sure. Out of curiosity, though, where were you when he… when it happened?"

Elers placed the photo back in the shoe box and began gathering the other photos to return them to the box, also. "At work," he said. "Clete and I work for the same construction company, but on different projects. He had a day of vacation coming, so he took it that day—said he wasn't feeling well—and when I got home, he was dead."

One last hunch. "Did Clete by any chance mention—within, say, a week or so before he died—running into one of the old gang from the apartment building?"

Elers shook his head. "Huh-uh. Why?"

"No reason." Actually, I was almost certain that Clete Barker had run into someone from his past, and that he'd died as a result of it.

I got up from the table. "I'd better get going," I said. "You've been very helpful, Mr. Elers, and I hope you won't mind if I call you if any other specific questions come up."

Elers rose and walked me to the door. "Sure," he said. "Any time."

We shook hands at the door, and I walked out into the glaring sunlight. It was going to be another hot day.

*   *   *

The exact address was 2012 Hutchins, and it was exactly as Elers had described it. It sat just far enough back from the street to have a small front yard edged with a neatly-trimmed, low hedge. A gray-haired man in walking shorts and a short-sleeved green shirt was washing windows on the ground-floor level, to the left of the centered entry door.

"Excuse me," I said, going up the walk until I was parallel with him and he could easily see me without turning around.

"Can I help you?" he asked, wiping the squeegee on a rag he took from his back pocket.

"I hope so," I said. "I've been admiring this building for years, and I wondered if there might be an apartment for rent."

"I'm afraid not," he said, bending over to take a sponge from a full bucket of water at his feet. "This building's a condo, anyway."

"Really?" I was surprised. "I had some friends who lived here a couple of years ago, and they were renting."

"That's possible," the man said, going on with his work while he talked. "It only went condominium about…oh, a little less than three years, I guess."

"You live here?"

"Yep. Right here." He tapped the window with his squeegee. "I was the first buyer, as a matter of fact."

"Well, then," I said, playing a long shot, "maybe you know my friends: Gene Harriman and Kyle Rholfing?" drawing two names out of a mental hat.

The man shook his head. "Afraid not. The building was totally vacated and renovated before it went condo. All the former tenants were gone when I first found the place."

Damn! "Any idea who owned the place before you bought in?" I asked, hopefully.

"Nope." He tapped on the window again with the squeegee, using the edge this time, and another man, slightly younger, appeared and opened the casement, giving me only a cursory glance. "Get me some more water, will you, Gregg?" the older man said, pouring the bucket's contents carefully along the hedge and handing the now-empty bucket through the open window. His friend took it and disappeared into the depths of the apartment.

"Still only eight units?" I asked.

"Yeah—two to a floor. Say, if you're interested in a condo,

you might try Elsinore Condo Corp.—they're the ones who did over this place, and they specialize in smaller, better buildings."

"Thanks," I said. "Thanks a lot." I turned and walked back to the street just as the younger man reappeared at the window with a fresh bucket of water.

*　*　*

All the way to my office, I couldn't get that building out of my mind. Eight apartments, seven deaths. Eight apartments, seven deaths. There was something there, other than the obvious implication that the eighth apartment belonged to the murderer. Rholfing had said something…some sort of warning signal I should be acting on, but wasn't.

Rholfing had been stretching the truth somewhat when he said he'd had the "penthouse" apartment—unless you could consider the top floor of any building as being a penthouse. But there was something else…about the penthouse apartment… *'with a delightful boy named Herb-something.'*

That's it! Rholfing had a roommate! Which meant one of two things: either Herb-something was a prime suspect or he could well be the next victim! The case for him being the killer rested largely on my own prejudice: I could see how anyone living with Rholfing might develop homicidal instincts; but I knew that was just fanciful thinking on my part. The question was how in the hell could I track him down. And if he were not the killer, and assuming he were blithely unaware of what was going on, what if the killer found him? Could he possibly be the hot number with the poodle Elers had mentioned? No. Rholfing lived on the top floor; Elers said the kid lived on the ground floor.

Shit! I didn't even have a last name to go on!

The first thing I did on getting to the office—after opening the window as wide as it would go—was to look up and call the Elsinore Condo Corp. If I could track down the building's former owner…

I was right in thinking Elsinore Condo Corp. wouldn't give

me any information on the property's former owner. It was getting too late in the day to try to make it to the Hall of Records to start a search through volume after volume of Trust Deeds and Land Titles, but I swore to get down there the minute they opened the next morning.

When I checked with my answering service and learned I had had three calls from a Mr. Tim Jackson, my heart fell into my stomach with an almost audible splash. I dialed Tim's office immediately, only to be told by whomever answered the phone that Tim was tied up with an autopsy. I hoped against hope that I didn't know on whom the autopsy was being performed. But my stomach told me I did. I left my number, then just sat down at my desk and stared out the window.

*   *   *

My watch indicated that more than an hour had passed when the phone rang, but my mind had been much too busy to notice the time. I felt like a greyhound at the dog races—no matter how fast I went, the rabbit went faster.

"Hardesty Investigations," I said, picking up the phone.

"Dick? Tim. Sorry to took so long to get back to you, but I had to wait until I could get away from the building. It's my turn for some bad news…"

"Herb-something," I said, flatly.

There was a pause from Tim's end, then: "Herb Lopez. How in the hell did you know?"

"Tim," I said, "don't ask. I'll fill you in later. Just give me the when and where."

"They found him this morning, but he's been dead at least three weeks—the body's in pretty bad shape, as you can imagine in this weather. Found at home by his parole officer. It seems Lopez had served at least two terms for sex offenses."

"Great."

"Any idea how many more we can expect?" Tim asked.

"No, Tim, I don't," I answered. Eight murders, eight apartments. But Rholfing and Lopez had been roommates. Maybe they *all* had roommates! Dozens of roommates;

thousands of roommates all just waiting for a hit from that magical, mystical amyl bottle. *Fuck*!

I tore my mind away from this cheery line of speculation and forced myself to concentrate on the issue immediately at hand. "Do you have Lopez' address and the name of his parole officer?" I asked.

"I knew you were going to ask," Tim said, "so I wrote them down. Lopez lived at 417 Bushnell; his parole officer's name is Brown—Ray Brown."

I wrote the information on a scratch pad. "One more thing, Tim," I said. "You saw all the bodies, right?"

"Right."

"Was any of them—and I'm thinking specifically of Lopez, Arthur Granger, or Gene Harriman—about five-ten, slender, very good-looking, medium-brown hair, with ice-blue eyes?"

"Nnnnnno…huh-uh; none of them. Granger wasn't bad looking, but not what you'd call overly attractive—he had a black beard and brown eyes. Harriman comes closer, but his eyes were brown, too, as I recall, and he was only about five-six. Lopez's a Latino: black hair, mustache, brown eyes, stocky. Who's the guy you're talking about?"

"You have two pretty fair choices," I said. "Either the next victim, or the murderer."

Tim gave a long, low half-whistle. "Jesus."

"I couldn't have said it better," I said. "Thanks, Tim. I'll be talking to you soon. You'd best get back to work."

Tim sighed. "Yeah. Take care of yourself."

"You, too, Number-One," I said as he hung up.

Now, I'm not all that much into stereotypes, but from what Elers had said about the shy kid with the ice-blue eyes, I had a hard time imagining him as a killer. Still, I'd been around long enough to know that a lot of very sick minds live inside attractive, sometimes beautiful, heads. And whoever rented the hotel room in which McDermott was killed had registered as "B. Kano," the kid's dog, which was pretty strange in itself.

Eight deaths, a shy kid with ice-blue eyes, and a poodle named Big Kano. It was a lot more than I had when I started. The question was: was it enough?

CHAPTER 9

Ed's call, some ten minutes after I arrived home, caught me just as I was stepping into the shower. I left the water running while I answered the phone.

"How's it going, Sam Spade?" Ed asked, and the sound of his voice helped relax me almost as much as the anticipated shower.

"Not to be believed, my lad, not to be believed," I said. I thought for a second about professional ethics and about my lifelong habit of not dragging other people into things that didn't concern them. But, damn it, I felt like talking, and I felt like talking to Ed. "Remember your offer to lend an ear any time I needed it? Well, I sure could use it now. And I think I mean it this time."

"You've got it. Your place or mine?"

"How about mine, if you don't mind? I'm just getting into the shower, so keep ringing the bell until I hear it."

"Well, if might be about an hour before I can get there," he said. "I've got a few things to do around here first."

"That's okay," I said. "I'll probably still be in there."

Ed laughed. "Okay. I'll be over as soon as I can."

"Ciao," I said. I put the receiver back on its cradle and went directly to the shower.

*   *   *

The dog. It had something to do with the dog, right? Let's say somebody killed the kid's dog ...*poisoned* it! Aha! The kid doesn't know who did it, but he knows it was somebody in the building, and he vows to get even. A shy kid? Still waters run deep. So he systematically kills eight people.

Great story, but just a trifle far-fetched. Why wait almost four years? Does it really make any sense to think that someone would kill seven innocent men just to get an eighth who might ...*might*! ...have killed his dog?

Stranger things have happened, but it just wasn't logical. There had to be something more to it.

Suppose it wasn't the kid at all? Suppose the kid's out there somewhere right now, all innocent and shy and blue-eyed and somebody's ringing his doorbell right this minute with his hand in his pocket holding onto an amyl bottle...

Somebody was ringing my doorbell. Ed already? It seemed like only five minutes since I'd hung up the phone. I turned off the water, yelled "Just a minute," and grabbed for a towel. A quick glance at the clock on my dresser showed that either the clock was off by over an hour, or I'd lost all sense of time again. Knowing me and showers, I opted for the latter.

Semi-dry, I wrapped the towel around me and padded to the front door, opening it to find Ed leaning against the frame, a finger poised over the doorbell.

"Come on in," I said. Ed followed me into the living room. "Too early for a drink?" I asked.

"It's never too early," Ed said, grinning.

"Good. Why don't you do the honors while I finish drying off and get dressed? Bourbon's over there, seven's in the fridge."

I did a quick blow-dry of my hair and slipped into a pair of jeans while Ed made the drinks. When I returned to the living room, Ed was sitting on the couch, looking through a month-old issue of 'Time.'

"I see here that somebody's shot President Lincoln," he said as I walked over to join him. He set the magazine down, picked up my drink from the coffee table, and handed it to me. "It's probably a little strong, but I figured you could use it."

I tasted it. He was right. "You forgot the seven," I said.

I sat beside him and took a long swallow, draining nearly a third of the glass.

"That bad, huh?" Ed said.

"That bad," I agreed.

"Well, I brought both ears. Any time you're ready..."

*   *   *

I told him everything, from the minute Rholfing first swished into my office to the minute he—Ed—rang the doorbell. When

I'd finished, Ed just sat there, quietly, looking at me. Finally, he got up, took both our now-empty glasses, and went to make us another drink.

"That," he said from the kitchen, "is some story. Where do you intend to go from here?"

"Tomorrow to the Hall of Records," I said, talking a little louder so he could hear me. "Then to whomever owned the building. From there on, it's anybody's guess."

Ed returned to the living room and handed me my refilled glass. "What about the police? Don't you suppose they'll solve the whole thing eventually?"

I took a sip of the drink and set it on the coffee table. "I sincerely doubt it," I said. "Do you realize how many unsolved murders take place in this town every year, even when the police are really trying to solve the case? With gay murders, let's be charitable and just say that their usual enthusiasm in pursuing justice is somewhat tainted with homophobia. And even if they were doing their very best, they think it's some homophobic serial killer just randomly murdering faggots, which makes the odds of finding him astronomical. I don't think he's a homo-phobe, and I don't think the killings are random. I'm sure he knows exactly what he's doing…I just don't know why. You can't find what you're not looking for, and from everything I can gather, the police are not looking for a link between the victims…at least, they're not looking hard enough."

"You could always tell them," Ed said, logically.

"Yes, I could. But why should I? At least right now. If I were to tell them what I know, who's to say they'd follow up on it properly? And it's almost guaranteed they'd do everything in their considerable power to see to it that I got off the case and stayed off. I'd probably be arrested for obstructing justice for not identifying myself after I found Rholfing, and just as probably lose my license. I've had a couple of professional encounters with the police before. I know how they operate. No, I'd rather go the whole distance on my own. Then we'll see what happens."

We sat in silence for a moment. "You know," I said, "one

of the frustrations in all this is not having a single real suspect—except possibly the shy kid with the poodle. If this were a detective novel or a movie, there'd be suspects coming out of the woodwork."

"What about me?" Ed asked. "Wouldn't I qualify?"

I shrugged. "Oh, sure. You. For having a phone number. Or Gary Miller, for being tired of being cheated on. Or Martin Bell, out of unrequited love for Arthur Granger. Open the phone book and pick out a name. But did anyone I've talked to know all eight men—and know them when they lived in that particular building? Did you?"

Ed shook his head. "I see what you mean," he said.

I shrugged again. "The prosecution rests. But thanks for the offer."

Ed reached over and put his closest hand on my leg, easily, casually. "Well, if I can't be a suspect, is there anything I can do to help?"

"You're doing it," I said. "At the risk of sounding maudlin, it means a lot just to be able to talk to someone."

"You can always talk to Tim," he said, half teasing.

"You know what I mean," I said, and immediately wished I hadn't.

"I know," he said quietly, then quickly took a long drink.

We sat in embarrassed silence for a minute or so, and I found my mind, as always, wandering back to the case. "If only I knew …" I said aloud.

Ed looked at me. "Knew what?"

"About the kid with the ice-blue eyes. Who the hell is he? *Where* is he? Is he the murderer, or the next victim?"

"You'll find out," Ed said, reassuringly.

"I hope so," I said. "I dread the thought of getting another phone call from Tim. I've got to find that kid, one way or another. I'd hate to think somebody else might die because I goofed, somehow."

Ed set his drink down, reached over and took me by both shoulders, turning me toward him. "Now, look," he said, his voice and face serious, "I don't know you well enough yet to butt into your affairs. But I know damn well you can't blame yourself for Rholfing's death, or for anything concerned with this case. You're doing the best you can, and I know you'll have all the answers soon. Just stay detached. They'll come. I know it."

"Thanks, coach," I said, grinning sheepishly. "I really appreciate it, and that's no bullshit."

Ed grinned and released me. "That's the boy," he said. "Oh," he added, "I nearly forgot—not to change the subject, which might be a good idea anyway—but I've got to make a trip to Chicago for a couple of days. We've just opened our new facility at O'Hare, and there are some bugs with the VIP lounge. They've been after me to come out there and take care of things, and I've been putting it off."

"When are you going?" I asked, surprised by my negative gut reaction to his news. I didn't want him to go, damn it. *Oh, come on, Hardesty, you're not fifteen anymore.*

Ed took another drink before answering. "Probably day after tomorrow, unless I can put it off again—which I doubt. I'll only have to be gone a couple of days, though. Should be back before the weekend. Think you can get along without me?"

"As Henry Higgins says, 'I've grown accustomed to your face,'" I said, "but I'll try to survive."

We both laughed, but I had the definite impression neither of us found it all that funny.

* * *

I was at the Hall of Records when the door opened the next morning. If you're ever looking for a fun way to spend the better part of a day, a trip to the Hall of Records isn't it. How anyone ever finds anything there is a wonder. It was well after lunch time—a fact attested to by the periodic rumbling of my stomach echoing through the vast chambers—when I finally found what I was looking for.

The property at 2012 Hutchins Avenue was purchased on June 16, three years previously, by the Elsinore Condo Corp.

from one Klaus Schmidt, 9312 Roosmeer Street, this city.

I returned the 50-pound ledger-type volume to the surly looking guy behind the desk who'd had his beady prison-warden eyes on me every minute lest I mark, mar, write upon, fold, staple, or otherwise mutilate the sacred documents. He obviously kept in shape toting the ponderous volumes back and forth from the stacks, but he had the vaguely haunted look of one who sensed microfilming was on the horizon, and that his job was in imminent—that is, within ten or fifteen years—danger.

A check of the phone directory in the library's main hall showed no listing for a Klaus Schmidt. Damn! My stomach was growling and muttering—I knew I should have had breakfast before I left the apartment—but it would just have to wait. 9312 Roosmeer was much more important right now, because 9312 Roosmeer would hopefully hold Klaus Schmidt who would, in turn, hold the final key to eight deaths.

* * *

9312 Roosmeer was a construction site. Girders and beams and cranes were casting long shadows over what remained of a quiet residential neighborhood of solid, stolid, early-part-of-the-century working-class homes. It's a good thing I've always hated to see a grown man cry, because I considered that possibility for a split second.

The site occupied a good half of the block, but five or six houses still remained, looking as though they were being shouldered out of the way—which, in fact, they were. I chose the house closest to where 9312 would have been, and knocked on the front door.

A little old lady, her hair in a bun and wearing—I swear—a black knit shawl over her neat but shapeless black house dress, appeared at the locked screen door. She looked like an ad for Ellis Island.

"Yesss?" she asked, inspecting every inch of me from top to bottom.

"Excuse me, ma'am," I said, for some reason feeling like a

twelve-year-old paper boy trying to make a collection, "but I'm trying to locate Mr. Klaus Schmidt, who used to live at 9312. I wonder if you could help me?"

Her face, which had been a study in suspicion, suddenly burst into a full-sunrise smile. "Klaus? You are a friend of Klaus Schmidt?"

"Well, not exactly," I said. Then, taking a cue from her reaction, I added: "But I understand he is a wonderful man."

"Vonderful? Vonderful? Klaus Schmidt iss a saint! Forty-two years Klaus Schmidt lived on this street and forty-two years he iss best friend to my dear Otto, bless his memory." I sincerely hoped she was blessing Otto's memory, and not Klaus Schmidt's. "Vot you vant from Klaus Schmidt?"

"I, ah…I represent a company that has a proposal Mr. Schmidt might find interesting—and very profitable," I lied. "Do you know how I could get in touch with him? It's really very important."

She looked me over again, slowly, from head to toe, then back again. Apparently making a satisfactory conclusion, she nodded her head once, curtly. "Sure," she said, decisively. "Sure. You vait here. I get you hiss address."

I watched through the screen door while she moved from the small, cluttered-but-neat living room to the archway-adjoined dining room. Opening the top drawer of a solid-looking, hand-carved mahogany credenza, she searched through it for a moment, then came up with an envelope. Holding it in front of her like a lady in waiting with a fan, she brought it to me, unlocked the screen and opened it just wide enough to hand the envelope to me.

"This I got from Klaus last veek. Ve write often, now that my Otto iss gone."

I took the envelope from her and looked at the return address: 4851 W. Winchester, Chicago, Illinois.

"He liffs now in Chicago," the old lady said. "Two years ago now he sells his house here. Klaus iss getting old; he vanted to be near his niece."

"He lives with his niece, now?" I asked.

Her laugh was warm and rich, not at all what I might have expected. "Ach, no! Klaus, he liffs mit no-one! He iss much too …how iss the vert…independent. He hass hiss own house there, ya, but near enough hiss niece so she can look after him."

"Do you know if he has a phone? Perhaps I could call him."

She shook her head. "Nein, nein. Klaus cannot hear so good any more. No phone."

"How about his niece?" I said, hoping. "Would you know her number—or her name?"

The old lady thought a moment. "Mueller. Krista Mueller. But her husband's name I do not know, and for sure vere they liff I am not certain."

There were probably ten pages of Muellers in the Chicago phone book, I was willing to bet. Still, I had Schmidt's address. The key was almost in my hand. I hoped!

"Thank you so much, Mrs…" I looked at the envelope "…Breuner. You've been a great help." She opened the screen door again and extended her hand for the envelope, which I returned to her.

"You vill go to see Klaus?" she asked.

She was one step ahead of me, but she was right. "Yes," I said. "I think I will."

"You giff him a big hello from me, you hear?"

"It'll be a pleasure," I said, backing away from the screen door. "Thanks again."

She smiled her goodbye, locked the screen door, and disappeared into the house.

*   *   *

"Chicago?" Ed said, and I hoped I detected more than a little enthusiasm in his voice. "You're kidding! That's great! Tell you what…let me pull a few strings around here, call in a few favors owed. Maybe I can get you a comp flight."

"Hey, no!" I said, hoping I sounded convincing. "I don't want to cause you any trouble, Ed. That's not why I called."

Ed was, fortunately, insistent. "Look, buddy, I haven't

worked fourteen years for Pan-World not to be entitled to a few perks. Just leave it to me. We can probably go on the same flight, if that's okay with you."

"Sure," I said. "I'd really like that. You're sure it's no…"

"Just leave it to me, I said. You want to come by my place tonight? I should be home around six."

I glanced at my watch. It was already four-thirty. "Great," I said. "I'll just have time to run home and change. I must smell like a laundry bag full of dirty sweat socks by now. I'll see you about six, then. S'long."

It sure is nice to have friends in high places, I thought as I hung up. Still, I felt a little guilty. I really hadn't meant to impose on Ed's position with the airline. But I was glad he'd offered. God knows I needed to get out of town, even for a day, and the prospect of traveling with Ed didn't exactly sour my mood.

I was just getting ready to leave for home when the phone rang. Hoping it wasn't Tim with news of another body, I picked up the receiver. "Hardesty Investigations."

"Hi, handsome." Tim sounded reassuringly cheery. "It's me, but don't worry; your blue-eyed friend hasn't shown up. Just thought I'd pass on the latest poop. Lopez' death still leaves the cops standing firmly on Square One. They haven't come up with a single thread connecting the victims other than their all being gay. I get the impression they're all holding their breath for the murders to stop so they can slam the whole thing into the 'unsolved' file and get on with meeting their parking ticket quotas."

I ran my hand through my hair, wiping the sweat off my forehead in the same motion. "They're not the only ones holding their breath," I said.

"Anything new from your end?" Tim asked.

"Yeah," I said. "A lot, finally. I'll fill you in on the details later, but I may be going to Chicago for a day or so. All eight of the victims lived in the same building about four years ago. I tracked down the owner of the building and he's living in Chicago. He's an old guy and apparently deaf, so the only way to find anything out is to go there and see him in person." I omitted mentioning anything about Ed, his offer, or the prospect of our traveling together.

"I'll keep my fingers crossed," Tim said.

"Do that," I said sincerely. "And I'll call you the minute I get back to town."

"Hey…" I waited through Tim's pause, and appreciated the sincerity in his voice when he finished the sentence: "…you take care of yourself, hear?"

"Thanks, Tim. I will. Talk to you soon." I hung up and left for home.

* * *

"It's all set," Ed said as he handed me a drink and sat down beside me. "I hope you don't mind my doing all this without checking with you, but we're right at the peak of a rush period, and I didn't have much choice." He looked at me for approval, and I gave a simple 'lead the way' gesture with one hand. He looked relieved. "Good. Anyway, we catch the 12:15 tomorrow, do a quick stopover in Omaha, and get into O'Hare at 6:22. If you wouldn't mind our staying together…" he looked at me again, and I just shook my head and grinned "…the airline has an arrangement with a couple hotels, so we could stay for practically nothing. You prefer the airport area or downtown?"

I shrugged. "Whichever," I said. "Pick one."

Ed gave me a quick, embarrassed grin. "I already did," he said. "The Wellington Inn on the near north; it's new and it's my favorite. But I'd have changed it if you'd had anything specific in mind."

We each took a belt from our drinks, then sat in comfortable silence for a minute or two.

"So what happens when you find him?" Ed asked, finally.

"Who?" I asked, puzzled. "Klaus Schmidt, the kid with the ice-blue eyes, or the murderer—assuming we're talking about three people rather than just two?"

Ed took another drink. "The killer."

I sighed and stared into my glass. "That depends…"

"On what?"

"Well, on whether I really do find the killer, for one thing."

"You will," Ed said, confidently.

I nodded. "Yeah, I suppose I will. In that case, it depends on the situation—whether I ever actually come face to face with him or not. Look, getting a name is one thing; finding the guy it belongs to might be another problem—he could be anywhere. And then actually proving that he did it… Obviously, the thing to do is the minute I get his name, turn it over to the cops and let them take it from there. But if I were to do it that way, I'd probably never find out why he killed those guys, and I really want to know. I'd like to at least talk to the guy, if I could."

"Did you ever consider that might be kind of dangerous?" Ed asked, watching me.

I grinned again. "Yeah. I guess it might."

"Well," Ed said, "this might be pretty presumptuous on my part, but if you need any help when the time comes, I'd sort of like to be there."

I met his eyes and locked on them. "Thanks," I said.

"You're welcome," he replied.

Ed's hand was resting on my leg, and I found myself reacting, as I almost always did, to his touch. He looked down at my crotch and smiled. "I think I know how I can help you with at least one of your immediate problems," he said.

"Yeah?" I asked, knowing the answer full well. "How's that?"

He proceeded to show me.

*   *   *

The flight to Chicago was smooth, on time, and thoroughly enjoyable. For Ed, it was like a family reunion. He spent almost half the flight joking with the stewardesses—and with the stewards, at least one of whom was, I got the definite impression, something more than a casual acquaintance. As an airline employee traveling on company business, Ed couldn't drink, but he saw to it that I was pleasantly high by the time the plane touched down at O'Hare.

I was all for taking a cab to the hotel until Ed pointed out just how far O'Hare is from downtown Chicago and suggested we take an airport bus, which would drop us off right in front of the hotel. We took the bus.

The Wellington Inn, as I might have guessed from knowing Ed even the short time I had, could have been designed with him in mind. Modern without being garish, comfortably elegant without being snobbish, efficient without being impersonal, it was what a hotel should be and so few are. Our room, on the 28th floor, overlooked a good part of the city. The fact that it had a single king-size bed wasn't lost on me, though Ed feigned mild surprise. I had, in fact, the impression that this whole thing had been set up for my benefit, and I was duly flattered.

We hadn't discussed my return flight, though with luck I could wrap up my business with Klaus Schmidt—and, hopefully, the entire case—the following day. My excitement at the prospect of finding the kid with the ice-blue eyes and the killer made me uncharacteristically hyper, and I was vaguely annoyed with myself for having such a good time in the process.

After we'd unpacked, Ed suggested we have dinner at his favorite Chicago restaurant—a place called the Carriage House.

He could have suggested McDonald's and it would have been all right with me.

A quick (for me) shower took care of whatever remained of my booze high from the plane, but didn't do all that much to calm me down. Thoughts were flashing through my mind like fireworks, all coming and going with such speed and in such disarray I couldn't make any sense of any of them. Rholfing; Tex/Phil; the painting of Gary Miller and the actuality of Gary Miller; a dog named Big Kano; Brad, the tattooed day manager at the El Cordoba; the phone number that led to my meeting with Ed; the kid with the ice-blue eyes; everything zipping, whizzing, and spiraling through the night sky of my mind.

"How do you do it?" Ed asked, looking at me from the corner of his eye as he made clean, smooth paths through the shaving cream on his face with deft strokes of his razor.

"Do what?" I asked, rubbing myself vigorously with a towel.

Ed rinsed his razor briskly in the hot water flowing from the sink faucet. "Stay in there so long and not come out looking like a prune," he said, returning his eyes to the mirror and the progress of his shave.

"I think someone in my family was part duck," I said. "Besides, showers are my only vice. This one was practically an in-and-out."

Ed snorted and swept the last remaining swath of shaving cream from his face. Leaning closer to the mirror and jutting out his chin, he made a careful visual and fingertip inspection of his cheek, chin, and neck. A quick frown announced the finding of a few stray whiskers in the vicinity of his left sideburn, which he dispatched quickly with a few short strokes of the razor. Another finger inspection, a satisfied nod to himself in the mirror, and he was through.

"I called for reservations while you were in the shower," Ed said. "Think we can make it in forty-five minutes?"

"How far is it?"

"Three blocks."

"We'll make it," I said.

We did.

*   *   *

The Carriage House turned out to be just that—a small but very nice little restaurant in a converted carriage house behind a former mansion now used as offices by several prestigious law firms. The whole place sat exactly sixteen people; the ground floor also held a small bar with six stools. We had to wait about forty-five minutes, then were led upstairs to our table. The clientele, though mixed, was predominantly what Tim refers to as "Our People."

We ordered a bottle of wine while we looked at the menu and, when the waiter had left with our order, I raised my glass in a toast. "To tomorrow," I said.

Ed raised his glass and touched it to mine. "To many

tomorrows," he amended.

Neither of us said anything for a few moments, but looking at Ed's face I could tell he had something he wanted to say.

"Something the matter?" I asked.

He looked at me and smiled. "No; not really... Well, I don't know."

He had me puzzled. "So talk," I said. "God knows I've done enough of it in the past several days."

I'd never seen Ed look like that before—his face reflected a mixture of doubt, determination, and trouble. I waited for him to say something, but he didn't for a long minute. Then he heaved a deep sigh and plunged in.

"Dick, I've been thinking about this for a long time now—since shortly after I met you, as a matter of fact; though I guess that hasn't been all that long, really, has it? Anyway...I know this may not be the right time or the right place...you have a lot on your mind right now; a lot of problems with this case you're on. I just want you to know that no matter how it turns out, I..." I watched him struggle with his words, and my stomach and chest were full of butterflies, "...damn it, Dick, I'm not some fluffy-sweatered, lint-brained little twink; I don't go bouncing around from one little faggot-novel romance to another. I don't gush, and I don't bullshit.

"I told you I've only had one lover in my whole life, and when I lost him, I swore to myself that I'd never have another. I don't ... *shit!*...I don't quote 'love' unquote you...you can't love somebody until you really know them and we just haven't known each other that long yet. But, damn it, I like you better than anybody I've met in a long, long time. Since Glenn. I care about you. I don't know why, but I do, and you've got to believe that." Abruptly, he picked up his glass and drained it. "I just wanted you to know," he said.

My ears heard him, but my head felt as though it were a balloon on the end of a long, long string. I tried to say something, but nothing came out. Finally, I did manage a typical Hardesty bit of wisdom. "Wow," I said, and drained my glass.

I poured us both another glass of wine. I could tell Ed was

almost excruciatingly embarrassed, but I kept my eyes on his face. He had trouble meeting my eyes, but after several tentative split-second contacts, our eyes finally locked on each other.

"I didn't do that very well, did I?" Ed said, with a quick, weak little grin.

"You did it just great," I said. "I couldn't have done it better myself…and I would have said exactly the same thing." I hadn't felt this giddy since I made it with the captain of my high school swimming team in a corn field when I was fifteen. "I'm not a gusher or a bullshitter, either. I'm not much of a talker, when it comes right down to it. Let's just say I feel we're going in the right direction, and I'll be damned happy to go just as far with you as either of us wants to go. Deal?"

Ed smiled, and I felt the same way I did when Gary Miller smiled at me—only Ed's was even better. "Deal," he said.

CHAPTER 10

I was awake, as always, at six thirty. Ed was dead to the world, though he'd left a wake-up call for seven o'clock with the front desk. I lay there beside him, staring at the ceiling, searching for faces in the blown asbestos as I'd done with clouds when I was a kid. I wanted a cup of coffee and a cigarette, but the comfort of being where I was outweighed my urge to get up.

I found myself watching Ed sleep—my eyes moving slowly over his hair, his face, his neck, down his chest, partly exposed where he'd tossed back the covers in his sleep. And I had the strangest sort of ache in my chest. I'd always thought Ed was handsome, but as I watched him sleeping, I suddenly realized I thought he was beautiful.

Ed rolled over in his sleep and draped one arm across my chest, making strange little animal noises that made me think of a hibernating bear. At seven o'clock sharp, the phone rang and I reached over to answer it.

"Good morning," the operator said in her professionally cheery voice before I'd had a chance to say anything. "It's seven o'clock. Today will be clear; temperatures will range in the mid seventies. Have a very pleasant day."

I grunted a "Thanks" and hung up. I was a little startled, when I glanced over toward Ed, to see his eyes wide open, staring at me.

"Jeez, Mack, I must'a really been smashed last night. I don't remember anything. Where the hell am I?" he said with a grin.

I stared at him in mock seriousness. "A good line," I said. "Use it often?"

"No," he said, leaning over to give me a quick kiss, then turning on his back and stretching, "but I've heard it a couple times."

"You, me, and the rest of the world," I said. "Come on, Sleeping Beauty—you said you're supposed to be at the airport before ten."

"We've got time," Ed said.

"Probably," I said, punching him in the arm, "but after last night, I'd kind of like to be able to stand up today."

Ed grabbed me in a bear-hug, growled, then pushed me back and rolled out of bed. "Yeah. Work, work, work." He padded into the bathroom and turned on the shower, then reappeared briefly in the doorway. "Me first," he said, indicating the shower with a jerk of his head. "Then you."

"Yowsah, boss," I said as he disappeared again.

*   *   *

"Any idea how I can get to 4851 Winchester?" I asked Ed as we finished breakfast in the hotel coffee shop.

Ed wiped some toast crumbs from the side of his mouth with his napkin. "Yeah …let's see…you could take a Lawrence Street bus west and get off at Winchester, I think. Or the Ravenswood El to Damon, then take a bus on Damon. It shouldn't be too hard; just check with the bus driver or the ticket booth on the El if you have any problems. Chicago's a pretty easy place to get around in, once you know the main streets. I've been here so often I feel like a native." He glanced at his watch. "Oh-oh! I'd better shag ass. I'll meet you here later this afternoon. Hopefully, I'll be done by around three."

I grabbed the check as he was reaching for it. "Go on—I'm going to finish my coffee. See you later."

Ed smiled, waved, and left.

*   *   *

4851 Winchester was what I was coming to think of as "typical Chicago" in architecture. Three stories high, set on a narrow lot with maybe four feet of space between it and its neighbors on both sides. Dark-red brick, enclosed porches, neat but tiny front lawn. Apparently a three-flat, with each apartment having its own entire floor. The mail box listed a P. Swietzer, a Weiler/Swanson, and K. Schmidt. No indication as to who occupied which floor.

On a hunch, I rang the bell on the separate door for the ground-floor flat, thinking as I did so that I might be engaging in an exercise in futility; if Schmidt were deaf, he probably couldn't hear the bell. But then I saw some movement behind a curtain in the bay that had once been the porch, and seconds later the door was opened by a wizened little man in a white shirt, baggy black pants and suspenders. A wire ran from his left ear to a lump in his shirt pocket, and he squinted at me through thick glasses.

"Yes?" he said, looking me over much as Mrs. Breuner had.

"Klaus Schmidt?" I asked, suddenly aware that my shoes probably needed polishing.

"Yes?" he repeated.

In deference to his hearing aid, I spoke a bit louder. "Mr. Schmidt, my name is Dick Hardesty. I'm a private investigator, and I'd like to talk to you for a few minutes about a building you owned up until about three years ago."

Schmidt intensified his squint, as though that made him hear better. "Yes?" he said.

I'd better try something ingratiating, I thought. "Oh, but before I begin, Mrs. Breuner, your former neighbor, sends her very best regards."

Schmidt brightened perceptibly. "Ah, yes? Anna! How is my dear Anna?"

"She's just fine, Mr. Schmidt, though she does miss you very much." Schmidt beamed. So far, so good. "Would you have a few minutes to talk to me?" I asked.

"Yes! Yes!" he said, stepping back from the door and opening it wide for me. "A friend of Anna's! How nice! Do come in, young man. Come. Come."

I followed him into the apartment, closing the door behind me. Like Mrs. Breuner's house, the apartment was small, neat, and cluttered with tangible memories. "You sit here," Schmidt said, stopping in front of an overstuffed chair. As I sat down, he shuffled into the adjoining dining room and dragged one of the chairs from the table into the living room. Positioning it directly in front of me, he sat down.

"Now you tell me about Anna," he said, his head bobbing gently in pleasure.

"Well, I'm afraid I don't know Mrs. Breuner very well," I said in one of my classic understatements. "I was mainly hoping you could tell me something about the building you owned at 2012 Hutchins Avenue. I'd like very much to know something about the people who lived there."

Schmidt looked momentarily confused, as if searching his memory. When he found what he was looking for, his face brightened again. "Oh, yes. Yes. A beautiful building. Beautiful."

"Yes, it is," I said. "It had eight apartments, is that correct?"

Schmidt thought, then nodded. "Eight. Yes. So nice a building. Such nice boys lived there. All of them. Wonderful tenants. Wonderful."

I felt my stomach beginning to tighten. "You remember them all, then?" I asked, hopefully.

Schmidt gave me a rather sad smile. "Yes. Sure. But you see, my memory, it is not as good as it was once. I am eighty-two this year. When the mind has eighty-two years of memories, some of them get lost now and then."

"Well, I'm thinking of people who lived in the building just before you sold it. Perhaps you could remember them. There was Kyle Rholfing, for example." I searched his face, watching as his thoughts washed over it in almost visible waves.

"Rholfing. Rholfing?" His lips and jaws moved as though chewing on the name.

"Blond…" I prompted.

"Oh, yes. Rholfing. So like a girl sometimes he was."

Good; one down.

"And Herb Lopez, Rholfing's roommate?"

Again, Schmidt thought. "Yes, Herbert Lopez. Him I did not know so well. He was a little strange, too, but not like Rholfing. Not like a girl. I think he liked sometimes the schnapps too well."

You're on a roll, Hardesty.

"And Alan Rogers, a painter?"

"Ummmmm. Yes. Him I remember. A nice boy. Nice. Very neat; I remember that. Very neat."

"Arthur Granger?"

"Arthur Granger?" he repeated.

"Yes, Arthur Granger. He had a beard."

Schmidt nodded. "Oh, yes. Like Mephistopheles he looked. A good tenant. Always paid his rent on time. Never late."

"Cletus Barker?"

Schmidt looked at me. "Big man? Never says a word?"

That fit Elers' description of him. I nodded. "Gene Harriman?" I pressed on.

Schmidt echoed my nod. "Gene Harriman. Yes."

"Arnold Klein?"

Removing his glasses, Schmidt tugged at the front of his shirt until he had worked enough of it loose from his pants to use as a cloth. He polished the glasses with it, held them up to the light, squinting; then, apparently satisfied, put them back on and tucked his shirt back into his pants. "Jewish boy," he said. "A good Jewish boy. Very nice."

I felt very much as though I were in a canoe being carried swiftly toward a waterfall. Every name brought be closer to the precipice. "Bobby McDermott," I said.

Schmidt nodded and smiled. "Such a one, that Bobby! Always late with his rent, but never could I be mad with him. He made me laugh; always with a joke, that one."

I could almost hear the roar of the falls. "Those were tenants of seven of the apartments, Mr. Schmidt. What I really need your help with is in finding out who lived in the eighth apartment."

Schmidt looked at me, blankly. "The eighth apartment?" he said. "The eighth apartment." Again, I could see his thinking process reflected on his face, which was going though subtle contortions as he tried to remember.

"The eighth apartment," he repeated.

"Granger, Rholfing, McDermott, Barker, Harriman, Klein, Lopez, Rogers, and…" I prompted.

Schmidt began rocking forward and backward, as he strained to remember. He also began to mutter to himself, softly, in German. His eyes were staring off into space, squinting as if to look for the answer. I said nothing, but my mind kept repeating *come on, come on!*

Finally, Schmidt stopped rocking and slapped both palms on his legs. "Nein!" he said, disgustedly. "No, it will not come. Growing old is a very angry thing sometimes. The mind will not tell you the things it knows. You tell me, I remember sure, but me remember by myself, nein. Ach!"

I'm not eighty-two yet, but I know exactly what he meant. I decided to try another approach. "About three years ago, not too long before you sold the building, something happened there," I began. "Something quite bad. Do you remember anything at all about it?"

Schmidt looked confused again. "I did not live in the building. I do not know everything that went on there…" But even as he said it, I could see that his eyes looked troubled, as though he were trying once again to remember.

"Whatever it was that happened," I said, "I think it involved a dog—a little dog named Big Kano."

A look of shock and recognition spread across Schmidt's weathered face. His eyes began to fill with tears, and he started to rock forward and back again. "Ach! Ach! Yes! Oh, yes! Sometimes, the mind it hides things from you that you should not remember. Tragic! So tragic!"

My throat was dry, but I managed to speak in spite of it. "Could you tell me what happened?" I asked, as calmly as I could.

Schmidt stopped rocking and looked at me, the tears still clinging to his lower eyelids. "So sweet a boy," Schmidt said, finally. "Such a wonderful boy. Like an angel, he was."

My arms, legs, neck, and shoulders broke out in goose bumps. "What happened?" I repeated.

"Dead. He killed himself. Ach! What a waste! What a waste! Such a boy!"

It took me a moment to calm myself down. "Did his death have anything to do with the dog?"

Schmidt nodded, and the act of nodding dislodged a tear which worked its way through the maze of wrinkles on his cheeks. "The dog, he runs out into the street. Such a small dog, the cars do not see him. He is killed. The boy, how he loved that dog! When the dog is killed, the boy goes into his apartment and he kills himself." Schmidt shook his head back and forth. "Ach! Such a waste! Such a waste!"

"The boy," I said. "What was his name?"

Schmidt waved his hand in front of his face, as though to chase away the memory. Then he shook his head again. "I cannot remember. I cannot think."

I heard my voice asking these questions, but it was as if I weren't really there. "Do you remember what the boy looked like?" I asked.

"Ya," Schmidt said. "How can I forget that face?"

"Was he tall, with brown hair?"

Schmidt nodded.

"And did he…" I was forcing the words out, now, "…have ice-blue eyes?"

Schmidt nodded.

I just sat there, my eyes focused on the old man but not really seeing him. I was thinking about the kid, the shy kid with the ice-blue eyes and no name, and I realized he'd become something of a romantic fantasy for me; someone I'd hoped I would find alive and who wouldn't have turned out to be the murderer. So much for fantasy. I thought briefly, then, of Ed and the reality that he represented. I realized that whatever it was I felt for him, he was worth a dozen fantasies. The kid was dead—Ed was here, and alive, and suddenly I wanted very much for things to work out for the two of us. It…

"Would you like maybe some coffee?" Schmidt's voice wedged its way into my thoughts, and I jerked myself back to reality and the present.

"If you have some made, that would be fine," I said, hoping he hadn't noticed my having wandered away, mentally.

Schmidt got up and shuffled into the kitchen, returning a few minutes later with two cups of coffee, minus saucers. He handed one to me and sat down again on the dining room chair. Suddenly, he made a move to get up. "You want cream and sugar?" he asked.

I waved him down. "No, black's fine. Thanks."

We drank our coffee and engaged in small talk heavily laden with Schmidt's reminiscences. His memory was obviously going the same way as his hearing, but he was an interesting, intelligent old man and, under different circumstances, I would have really enjoyed talking with him. As it was, my heart wasn't in it. I had one final question for Schmidt—if his answer was "no," it would mean I had reached a dead end in the case. I couldn't face up to that possibility, so I forced myself to concentrate on the conversation and the coffee.

But the inevitable, though it can be postponed, can't be avoided. Schmidt was obviously tiring, and the coffee was long gone. Reluctantly, I knew it was time. I made a show of looking at my watch. "I'm sorry, Mr. Schmidt," I said, "but I didn't realize what time it was. I've really got to be going." I got up, not quite sure what to do with my coffee cup, but Schmidt, rising slowly and with effort, reached for it once he was standing, and I gave it to him. I waited while he took the cups into the kitchen and returned.

"Oh, one other thing," I said as he walked me to the door. "About the young man who died…did he have a roommate?"

Schmidt paused in mid-shuffle. "Ya!" he said, his eyes widening. "Why I did not remember him? A nice man. A very nice man."

I suddenly wished I hadn't drunk the coffee—I could feel the caffeine eating away at my stomach lining. "Do you by any chance remember his name?" I asked, my fingers crossed.

We'd reached the door, and Schmidt had his hand on the knob. He again stopped in mid-motion, thinking. "Nein. No. I am sorry. I cannot remember."

"Do you recall what he looked like?" I asked.

Schmidt thought again, hand still frozen on the doorknob. "Tall," he said. "Very handsome. Dark hair. Very nice man. He and the boy, they were such good friends. It is very sad; very sad. Ach! What a pity."

Schmidt's description could fit any one of ten thousand guys I see on the street every day. *One final chance*, I thought. "Would you happen to have any records—any rent ledgers, anything like that—that might have all the tenants' names?"

Schmidt's face brightened. "Ya! Of course. In the basement I have them somewhere. I have not seen them in years, but they are there. Tomorrow when my niece comes over, I will ask her to look for them."

"I wouldn't want to put your niece to any trouble," I said, hoping I wasn't sounding too pushy. "Perhaps I could help you find them today, if you'd like."

Schmidt shook his head. "No, no. Krista, tomorrow she will look. I do not climb up and down stairs as well as I used to. And the basement, it is a mess. My tenants here, they are not so nice as my other tenants. Always they are leaving the basement unlocked. The neighborhood children, they love to go down there and play, and such a mess they make. They are only children, but I would not want them to hurt themselves down there. I tell my tenants: 'Keep the door locked so the children cannot get in,' but they do not remember." Schmidt opened the door. "Tomorrow afternoon you come back. We have some coffee and talk some more, all right?"

"I'll look forward to it," I said. At the sidewalk, I turned to wave goodbye, but Schmidt had already closed the door and disappeared.

*   *   *

Ed was waiting for me when I got back to the hotel. He seemed almost as nervous as I'd been earlier, so I hastily filled him in on everything that had happened. When I told him about the kid's being dead, he looked almost as sad as I'd felt when I'd heard about it. Maybe, from all I'd said about him, the kid had become Ed's fantasy, too.

"Hey, look," I said when I'd finished my minute-by-minute account of my visit with Schmidt, "since this case is going to come to a head tomorrow one way or the other, what say we go out on the town tonight and really celebrate? On me, this time."

Ed grinned and reached over to mess up my hair. "I'd love

to, sport, but…" he heaved a deep sigh, "…that German trade delegation—the one I think I mentioned right after we met—is on its way back home and is stopping over in Chicago. They're getting in at midnight and the company thought it would be very nice if, since I'm here and have worked with them before, I could be there to look after them during their layover. That's about the last thing I want to do, but that's also what they pay me for, so …"

"That's okay," I said. "We can still have dinner, though, can't we?

"That we can," he said.

And that we did, at a great steak house just down the block from the hotel. Ed left for the airport at about ten o'clock, and, at his insistence, I set off to make the rounds of some of the local bars. ("No point in just sitting around the hotel," he'd said and, while bars aren't my favorite places, I agreed.)

I've found out one thing about gay bars. If you're in a strange town and you're not much of a drinker and you're not out cruising, they can be pretty dull places.

I got back to the hotel just after midnight, not even high. I got undressed, turned on the TV, and climbed into bed. I must have dropped off to sleep like a rock, because the next thing I felt was the movement of the bed as Ed climbed in beside me. When I opened my eyes, the room was dark. I turned over and propped myself up on my elbows. "Welcome back," I said.

"Hey, I'm sorry," Ed said. "I didn't want to wake you."

"No sweat," I said. "How did it go?"

He shrugged. "Like always. They could have gotten along perfectly well without me. And how was your evening?"

I raised one forearm off the bed to make circles in the air with my index finger. "Whoopee," I said. "I took one good look at the toddlin' town and toddled right back here to bed."

I was suddenly aware that Ed's eyes were on me, and I turned to see him staring at me intently, as though he were trying to reach inside me with his eyes. "Dick," he said, not breaking his stare, "Do you remember what I said the other night at dinner?"

"You think I could forget?" I asked.

"Just checking," he said.

I reached over and put my hand on his shoulder. Ed moved toward me until the tips of our noses touched. I could hear him breathing, and could smell his warm, clean breath.

"I can't always say what I feel," I whispered, "but they say actions speak louder than words." I kissed him, long and deep, our tongues doing a slow thrust-and-withdraw between us. Finally, I broke off the kiss but let my tongue move over his chin and down his neck. He was breathing more heavily now, as I lapped his hardened nipples and slowly moved down to his belly button and beyond until I felt an insistent tapping on my chin, in time with his heartbeat.

There is a subtle but definite difference between lust and making love. I think Ed and I both knew which this was. I took my time, exploring every inch with my tongue, loving the feel and the taste, then moving my lips up, over and down. I tried to pace it, to make the pleasure, and the memory, last as long as possible. But soon I could sense his countdown beginning… Then there was a low groan and—*Liftoff!*

Neither of us moved for a full minute. Then he pulled me up to him and we kissed again.

Finally, he rolled me over and whispered, "Your turn."

* * *

At one-thirty that afternoon, I was walking up the sidewalk to Schmidt's building. I woke up at six-thirty as usual but managed to force myself back to sleep until nine. I woke Ed at eleven so he could get back to the airport. ("No rest for the wicked," he muttered as he staggered into the bathroom.)

I was strangely calm, which rather surprised me. If Schmidt's niece had found the records, I'd have my answers. The shy kid with the ice-blue eyes would have a name, and so would the murderer. It might take me some time to find him, but once I had his name, I knew I could do it.

A thin, pleasant-looking woman opened the door—Schmidt's

niece, apparently—and, when I introduced myself, showed me in. Schmidt was sitting in the overstuffed chair I'd occupied the day before, and on the floor beside him was a large cardboard box full of ledgers and manila folders labeled, in large, Germanic script "2012".

The old man smiled as I shook his hand, obviously happy to see me. I guessed he didn't get many visitors. "You've met my Krista?" he said, indicating his niece with a nod of his head. She and I exchanged smiles and nods.

Gesturing to a rocking chair in the bay window at the side of the room, Schmidt said: "Sit. Sit."

I pulled the rocker over to him as Krista disappeared into the kitchen.

Schmidt leaned forward, beckoning for me to do the same. "We have coffee and strudel," he said in a conspiratorial whisper. "My Krista, she makes a strudel the angels are jealous!" He sat back in his chair and we were quiet for a moment until Krista reentered the living room with a tray bearing two coffee cups—on saucers—and two dessert plates of rich-looking strudel.

"There," she said, drawing up a small stool and setting the tray on it, within easy reach of both Schmidt and me. "Now, you two men talk. I've got to see about the laundry." With another smile, she left the room.

The strudel was delicious. We ate it in silence, Schmidt's fork clicking on the plate as he rapidly cut the strudel into small pieces. Having done so, he much more slowly conveyed each piece of the pastry, with a slightly shaking hand, from the plate to his mouth with obvious delight.

When his plate was empty, he returned it to the tray. "My Krista is a treasure," he said. "In a museum she should be."

We talked idly for a few minutes, Schmidt telling me of his boyhood in Germany, his coming to the United States, and his life here these past sixty-eight years. The narrative was a bit fragmentary, with certain things, places, and people temporarily or permanently misplaced, but again I was aware of how much the old have to share, if only the young would listen.

My eyes, unfortunately, kept straying to the cardboard box.

My mind never left it for a second.

At last, Schmidt noticed my preoccupation with the box, and reached over to pick up the ledger laying on top. "The children," he said, "they opened the box, but this I think is what you are looking for."

He handed it to me, and I saw it was a hand-written listing of rent receipts from 2012 Hutchins Avenue for the period the two years before the building had been sold. I slowly turned the pages, my eyes sweeping up and down the neat columns.

Each apartment had its own listing, under the name(s) of its tenant(s). They were all there: Alan Rogers, Gene Harriman, Kyle Rholfing/Herbert Lopez, Bobby McDermott, Arnold Klein, Arthur Granger, Cletus Barker. I wanted to turn the pages faster, but somehow I couldn't. Seven apartments. Eight murdered men. The eighth apartment was the last in the ledger.

Come on, Hardesty! Turn the fucking page! my mind screamed at me, but my fingers were slow to respond. Aware that I was holding my breath, I turned the page.

It was blank.

Near the binding were the ragged edges of two pages which had been torn from the book.

CHAPTER 11

Of course, you stupid shit! my mind kept berating me all the way back to the hotel. *You think you're dealing with some sort of moron here? You think the murderer is stupid? He had to know someone would come after him sooner or later; he knew Schmidt would keep records. He's had—when was the first murder? Three months, at least. Three months to destroy those ledger pages—assuming he hadn't done so even before Schmidt moved to Chicago. You're back to square one, Hardesty. Square one!*

I left a trail of clothes from the door of the room to the bathroom. What I hadn't removed by the time I reached the shower I left in a heap in front of the tub.

Not quite square one, I thought as the warm spray began to beat against the tense muscles at the base of my neck. The first thing I'd do when I got back home would be to go to the library and check out every single obituary column in the local papers for all of the two years before the building was sold, if necessary. I'd find the kid's name, all right. Maybe see if I could get hold of electric/gas company records; or the phone company. Somehow I'd find out the kid's name, and who his roommate was and why eight men should have died over a dog.

It wasn't over the dog, of course—at least, not directly. It was because the kid killed himself. The murderer blamed everyone in the building, obviously. But why? Did one of them run over the dog? And would anyone in their right mind murder seven innocent men just to get at an eighth—a guy who'd probably accidentally run over a tiny dog he probably didn't even see? You can't kill eight people just because one poor, mixed up kid killed himself over a dog. And why wait three years? It…

Ed's knock on the shower door yanked me back to reality and scared the shit out of me. I turned off the water and opened the shower door. Ed was holding an armload of my discarded clothes.

"You leave an interesting trail," he said, grinning. When

he saw the look on my face, though, his grin faded. "What happened?" he asked.

I told him everything while I dried off. He listened, sober-faced, and said nothing until I'd finished.

"I'm really sorry," he said at last. "I was sure you'd have your answers by now; I really was. But I know you well enough by now to know that you'll keep on it until you have it solved. It's only a matter of time."

"Yeah," I said, putting on a pair of shorts. "Time. I've got lots of that."

"Look," Ed said, trying to cheer me up against pretty heavy odds, "I've wrapped up everything I had to do around here. We can head back home any time you like. Or maybe we could stay around Chicago for a few days, if you want. I've got some time-off coming; we could take a couple of days and just relax and enjoy ourselves, do the tourist bit—Chicago's really got a lot going for it, you know, and we haven't given it a chance."

I realized what he was trying to do, and I appreciated it a lot more than I could probably manage to tell him. "I don't know, Ed," I said. "It sounds good, but…"

"Well, look, then…let's just take it one step at a time, okay? Starting with tonight. Let's go out and do some serious relaxing. Then, in the morning, we'll see how you feel, and if you want to go back, we'll go back." He looked at me and extended his hand. "Deal?"

I took his hand and shook it. "Deal," I said.

"Good," he said. I plugged in the hair drier and began to dry my hair and watched in the mirror as Ed went into the bedroom and began emptying his pockets onto the dresser. Kicking off his shoes and unbuckling his belt as I turned off the drier, he said: "Now it's my turn for the shower. You finish getting dressed and we'll lay out our battle strategy as soon as I get out."

He eased by me and patted me on the rear as he got into the shower and slid the door shut. His attempts to bring me out of my funk were working, and as I watched him through the shower door, I got a tight feeling in my chest. *Damn it, Hardesty,* I thought, *just what do you feel for this guy?*

The problem was, I was pretty sure I knew, and I wasn't quite sure what I should do about it. I just stood there, staring at him through the closed glass door.

'Love'? Me? Loner Hardesty? Old 'I don't need anybody' Hardesty? In love with some guy I've known for all of three weeks, if that? Come on, now!

Well why the hell not, damn it? I was getting angry with myself by this time. Why the hell shouldn't I let myself care for someone who ob-…yes, damn it, obviously… cares for me?

I set the drier on the counter and went into the bedroom to get dressed while my mind carried on its increasingly heated debate. I took a pair of socks out of the dresser drawer and saw that Ed's billfold had fallen off the edge of the dresser and onto the floor, spilling business cards and papers all over.

Cursing myself, I knelt down to pick up the mess. Several photos had fallen out, as well, and curiosity got the better of me as I gathered them up. One was a very old photo of a man and woman standing beside a snow-covered car—Ed's parents, I surmised, probably before their divorce. An obviously newer one was of a little girl about three years old—probably one of his nieces. And one was of a young man, about twenty-five, with light brown hair and ice-blue eyes holding a small dog. The back of the picture said: 'To Ed with love always, Glenn and Big Kano.'

* * *

I was sitting on the edge of the bed, the billfold beside me, when Ed came out of the shower. His eyes went immediately from my face to the billfold.

"I didn't mean to pry," I heard my voice saying. "It fell off the dresser and everything spilled out…"

Ed, who'd stood momentarily frozen, the towel held at one shoulder, resumed drying himself. "It didn't fall: I deliberately dropped it." he said, his voice gentle. "I knew even before I went to Schmidt's last night that you wouldn't give up. When you mentioned searching through the obituaries and utility records,

I knew you'd find out sooner or later. I just decided that sooner would be better for both of us."

I stood somewhere in that vast room behind my eyes and looked out at him. My body was a robot, with somebody deep inside pushing buttons and levers to manipulate my movements. I knew I had to say something, but didn't know how to say it.

My mouth was so dry, I could hardly open it. I finally managed. "Why?" I asked.

Ed finished drying himself and sat down on the bed next to me, the towel draped across his lap.

"I met Glenn when he was twenty-two," he began, and even in my shocked state, I was impressed by how calm he was. "He was an orphan and he was an alcoholic. We had a very rough first year; because he was beautiful, he'd been used and abused since he was a kid. No one had ever loved him and he thought no one ever could. His drinking nearly destroyed us several times. But I finally convinced him to get help, and with A.A. and counseling, he quit drinking completely. He even came to believe that maybe someone could love him, and that maybe I did. I was so proud of him."

I could almost hear gears and wheels grinding as my head turned to look at Ed; to watch his face as well as to listen to his voice.

"On the first anniversary of his being sober—recovering alcoholics call it their 'birthday'—we went to Hawaii, and when we got home, I bought him a puppy. Glenn named him 'Big Kano,' after a beach we'd found in Hawaii. He was really crazy about that dog—it was the first one he'd ever had and I think he felt it was the first time he understood what unconditional love is.

"We moved into that building shortly thereafter. A gay friend at work had told me about it—he lived right across the street. The apartment was great, but the people...the people were something else." Ed had been staring off into space, but suddenly his eyes locked onto mine, almost as if they were pleading with me to believe him. "You know something about them," he said. "Every single one of them was a bastard in his own right.

Glenn…you've seen his picture, now. You know how beautiful he was. Well, he was that beautiful on the inside, too. He was sweet, and gentle, and loving, and kind. We were good for each other. We needed each other.

"The guys in the building, they knew that, but they never stopped with their passes; always hitting on me, or hitting on Glenn. They knew we were together, but they never stopped. They scared Glenn, sometimes. They just made me angry, but I tried not to let it show, since we all had to live together, sort of."

Out of the corner of my eye, I could see that Ed had begun to knead the towel, slowly, first one hand and then the other, unconsciously.

"I didn't travel much with my job in those days, and most of the time when I had to be gone for a few days, Glenn would go along with me. My friend across the street would look after Big Kano, though Glenn hated leaving him. Glenn never liked to be alone; he'd been alone all his life, he used to say, and now that he had me, he didn't like for us to be apart. He was making great progress, but he was still incredibly insecure.

"Then, one weekend I had to make a spur-of-the-moment trip to handle some minor glitch with some VIP arrangements. I asked Glenn if he wanted to go, but he'd made an appointment to take Big Kano to the groomers, and he said he'd stay home—it would only be for the weekend."

Suddenly aware of his kneading, Ed stopped and awkwardly smoothed the towel out with both hands.

"When I got the call telling me Glenn was dead, I flipped out. I couldn't get a flight for a couple of hours, but I couldn't wait, so I just rented a car and started driving back home—it was only about 250 miles. I didn't make it. I plowed into a freeway divider about fifty miles from home."

His voice was flat, now, and he stared at the towel as he talked, head down. His fists were clenched tight.

"I was three months in the hospital. Broken leg, cracked ribs, a concussion, not to mention, shall we say, 'emotional problems.' As soon as I was released from the hospital, the company sent me overseas—they were wonderful to me, considering everything. Nothing was said—nor has it ever been—about my being gay, though I'm sure it's no big secret. Anyway, I'm sure they sent me away to help me forget—which just goes to show how naive some people can be.

"My sister flew out from Detroit and handled Glenn's burial—the fact that I couldn't even go to the funeral made matters worse—and came back to stay with me right after I got out of the hospital. When I got news of the transfer overseas, she took care of the closing of the apartment and selling off most of the furniture. I don't know what I would have done without her help."

He was silent for a long moment, then gave a deep, unconscious sigh, and continued.

"I never really knew the details of what had happened, other than that Big Kano had been run over and that Glenn had gotten drunk and shot himself with the gun we kept to protect against burglars. I couldn't understand it—but, then, I couldn't handle it, either. Maybe I didn't really want to know, in a way."

I didn't know what to say. I wanted to say something …do something…but I didn't know what. So I just sat there, feeling hollow.

Taking a deep breath, Ed straightened up, consciously unclenched his fists, and turned to look at me. He tried to smile, but didn't quite make it.

"Shortly after I got back from Kenya this year, I went out for drinks with the friend who'd lived across the street from us—he'd just found out he'd gotten a permanent transfer to Honolulu and wanted to celebrate. We got a little drunk, and the subject of Glenn and me came up. He apparently assumed I knew what had really happened, and said how sorry he was and how he'd always wondered why I hadn't gone out and killed those bastards for what they did to Glenn." He rubbed one hand, hard, across his forehead. "It was like I'd been kicked in the stomach, but I asked him to tell me everything he knew, and he did. He'd gotten the story in bits and pieces from the guys involved, but it was all there.

"The minute I was out the front door that last weekend, Rholfing came up with the idea of having a 'building party' that same night. They'd never all been particularly chummy with one another, from what I knew, but I think Rholfing saw it as a good chance to get at Glenn—and so did everybody else. Naturally Glenn was invited, but I'm sure he didn't want to go. He knew what kind of creeps those sons-of-bitches were. He knew every one of them was just dying to get their hands on him.

"But Glenn never wanted to offend anyone, so he went. Like I said, he hated to be alone. Rholfing made a punch for the party. Every one of those motherfucking pigs knew Glenn was an alcoholic. Every one of them!"

Ed's face was flushed and it was obvious he was maintaining his control only with effort. I sat there, listening—not wanting to hear, but desperate to know. His eyes slowly moved to my face. I could see they were misted, and I was embarrassed for him.

"They spiked the punch," he said, his voice autumn-leaf dry. "They knew Glenn was an alcoholic, and they spiked the punch! They thought it would be 'cute' to get him drunk!"

Ed swiped quickly at his eyes with one hand and gave me a quick, embarrassed smile. "Sorry, Dick," he said, with a short sniff. "I know this sounds pretty melodramatic, but I haven't talked about this to another living soul—ever. Can you believe that?"

I believed it, and nodded.

Ed sat quietly for another moment, then continued. "Anyway," he said, "they got him drunk. Really drunk—which isn't all that difficult with an alcoholic who hasn't had a drink in over a year. And then, when he was drunk and they were all drunk, the party turned into an orgy. Glenn passed out and they gang-raped him. Every one of those God-damned faggots had a turn at him—even that cunt, Rholfing, somehow got it up long enough to fuck him."

He paused just long enough to take a long, deep breath, like a swimmer going down for a long dive. "Glenn had Big Kano with him— sort of for a security blanket, I guess. The dog must have started barking once they started in on Glenn, and one of those pricks put the dog out onto the back porch. Somehow, he went down the stairs and out into the street. A car hit him. The squeal of the car's brakes and Big Kano's yelp brought Glenn to. He went wild. He fought his way out of the apartment and down to the street. When he found Big Kano dead, he just turned and went back into our apartment and took out the gun I'd kept for protection and shot himself. I guess he thought I wouldn't understand; that I wouldn't love him anymore."

Sweat was running down Ed's forehead, but he didn't seem to notice. His voice was still almost conversational, but I could literally feel his anguish. He said nothing for quite a while, and I could see him regaining his composure.

"The house I rented in Nairobi was crawling with bugs and rats, and I hired a guy who worked in the Ministry of Agriculture and moonlighted as a fumigator. They still use pesticides the U.S. had banned a long time ago—and they still use cyanide for fumigation and rodent control. It did the trick, but a few days after I moved back in, I found a small canister of cyanide sitting on the floor of a closet. I called the guy who'd fumigated the house and he seemed very unconcerned. There wasn't very much in the can, and he suggested I keep it in case the rats came back. So I put it into an old prescription medicine bottle I had, clearly labeled it 'cyanide' and put it under the sink in the kitchen and forgot about it. When I came back to the States, it got packed with my other things and shipped back here. Customs didn't say a thing. I'd nearly forgotten I still had it, until… ." He shrugged.

"When I found out what had happened to Glenn, I went into a kind of shock, and it was only as I started coming out of it that the rage started to build up. I knew I wanted to kill them all, but it was still all just an internalized feeling and I didn't have any real plans as to how to actually do it.

"So one night I forced myself to go out to the bars, and who should I see but Alan Rogers. The minute I saw him, it was as though reality stopped and I was watching a movie; I've never had a feeling like it before, or since, thank God. He was fairly well drunk, and when he saw me staring at him, he came over and started putting the make on me. He didn't even recognize me at first, and when he did, it didn't seem to mean anything to him. It had been three years, of course, so he probably assumed—as apparently they all did—that either I didn't know what had really happened, or that I'd just shrugged it off. After all, it hadn't been that big of a deal for them; why should it have been for me?

"And then he took out a bottle of amyl and asked me if I wanted a hit. I heard myself telling him no, and watched him, in slow motion, unscrew the cap of the bottle, close one nostril with an index finger, and take a snort so deep I thought he would inhale the liquid right out of the bottle.

"That's when I got the idea. But, you know, I still don't know whether I would have gone through with it if he hadn't called me. I think now part of me gave him my number as a test. He flunked."

He looked at me again, and the corners of his mouth made subtle little quivering motions, as if he were trying again to smile and just couldn't make it. "It's ironic, isn't it? But if I hadn't given him my number, I wouldn't have met you. Funny how things work out."

Neither of us really thought it was.

We sat side by side on the bed; part of me wanted to reach out and touch him; part of me wanted to get up and run—not because I was afraid of him, but because I was afraid of me.

After an indeterminate amount of time, which might have been seconds or minutes, Ed finally spoke again.

"How much of this do you really want to know?"

"All of it," I said.

Ed nodded. "The very next morning before I left for work, Rogers called and asked me over. I told him I had to go out of town for a few days, which I did, and that I didn't feel right about our getting together, with him having a lover, and he laughed and said, 'It sure won't be the first time; and besides, what he doesn't know won't hurt me.' And that did it. I told him I'd talk to him when I got back, and he said 'Okay, I'll be just as hot then.' Can you believe that? I was giving him every chance to save his miserable life, even hating him as I did, and he blew it."

He sat there, shaking his head and staring at the floor where his wallet had been. "I did have a two-day trip to San Francisco scheduled; somehow I'd managed to get through my work assignments without anyone noticing anything, but inside I was a real basket case. Even then, I was thinking that if Rogers would lay off, I might be able to avoid doing what I knew had to be done.

"I had a little free time in San Francisco, and I went out shopping." he continued, "I went to a porno shop and bought three bottles of amyl. I found an army surplus gas mask and some good rubber gloves, and bought them, too. When I got home, I had two messages on my machine from Rogers. That did it.

"I dumped the amyl out of two of the three bottles I'd bought, and rinsed the bottles thoroughly. That night, I took the cyanide, the gas mask, gloves, solvent, and the bottles to the roof of my apartment building.

"I put on the gas mask and dropped a little of the powdered cyanide into the bottle, then carefully poured in acid solution and immediately capped the bottles tight. Instant gas chamber. It never really occurred to me that I could very well have killed myself if I'd made a mistake while doing all this, and I guess at the time it wouldn't really have mattered. All I could think about was Glenn and what they had done to him... Actually, I didn't realize until later that the combination of cyanide and sulfuric acid could have—and probably should have—blown the amyl bottle up and killed me in the process. But I was incredibly lucky, and it didn't. Maybe it was in the proportions of the cyanide to the acid, maybe the fact that I made such a small batch... Anyway, somebody up there was watching over me, and I never had a problem.

"Rogers called me the next day and asked me over. He said his lover would be gone all day. The sonofabitch had a lover and he was still a fucking whore!

"When I got there, he answered the door stark naked. He didn't give a shit about his lover, he didn't give a shit about me; all he wanted was another trick. The fucker didn't even say 'hello'—he just yanked his head toward the bedroom and I followed him in."

Ed stopped, dropped his eyes to the towel in his lap, and stared at if for a moment. Once again he gave a long, slow sigh before continuing.

"Anyway, I reached into my pocket, took out the amyl bottle, uncapped it carefully, held my breath, and shoved the bottle tightly under one of his nostrils. He reached up and closed the other nostril with his index finger and took a real deep hit. Then he just fell over backwards, and he was dead in seconds. I quickly put the cap back on the bottle, being careful not to spill any on my skin, and moved him around on the bed so it looked like he was sleeping, pulled the covers over him, and started looking for the slip of paper I had given him with my phone number. When I couldn't find it, I left and didn't look back.

"I thought later about photos or anything that might connect me to any of them, or any of them to each other, or to the building. I guess Rogers didn't have any, anyway, but I made it a point to find out with the others."

Ed sat up straight, rolled his shoulders up and back, then rotated his neck in a slow circle to relieve some of the tension in his muscles. I was still numb, and don't remember having moved— other than my head—from the moment he'd started to talk.

"I won't go into detail with the rest," he said, "except to say that having done it once, I had to keep going. I tracked them down, one by one." He shook his head, as if in disbelief. "I didn't care if anybody caught me or not; I didn't care if the cyanide killed me, too. I didn't care about anything, really."

He turned to face me, and his expression was one I'm not sure how to describe, but I saw something there that nearly tore my heart out. "And then I met you. And all of a sudden I cared about something again. I'd gotten everyone by then—everyone but Rholfing. Maybe I'd held him off until last because he was so repulsive to me I couldn't stand the thought of even looking at him. When I got to his place, I really thought the cops might be there; that he knew why I'd come. But he started chattering away about how he'd just talked to you and how surprised you'd be when you found out he remembered about the building and everybody who'd lived there. He knew Bobby McDermott was dead, of course, but I realized that he didn't know that everyone else was, too, and that he didn't connect me with McDermott's death at all.

"He just stood there, babbling away and looking like Madame Butterfly in that stupid kimono. I couldn't believe it. I just stared at him, and then brought out the amyl bottle. When he saw it, his eyes lit up and he said 'Ooooh, candy!' and practically grabbed it out of my hand. I started to say something, but he had the bottle uncapped and shoved under his nose before I could say a word. He closed one nostril with his thumb and took a deep snort. I'll never forget the surprised look on his face. I managed to grab the bottle out of his hand as he fell and kept it from sloshing all over the room. I knew you'd be over right away, so I split."

There was another pause, during which we both just there, not looking at one another.

"I went home, opened every window in the place, put on the gloves, and opened the bottle under the water in the toilet bowl. It was practically empty anyway. I put the cap back on underwater, then I flushed the toilet three or four times and that was it. I scrubbed out both the empty amyl bottles—I used the first one completely, put them in with the trash, and took it to the dumpster. Then I came back inside and called you.

"And here we are."

I forced myself to turn and face him. "And here we are," I repeated. "The next question is, what do we do now?"

Ed got up from the bed and sat on the edge of the dresser, facing me. "That," he said, bracing himself with his palms flat on the dresser top, "is up to you. But before you decide, I want you to know three things. One is that I had every intention of turning myself in to the police once they were all dead. I still will, if that's what you think I should do. I had decided that long before I met you; but, damn it, I have met you, and now I don't want to lose you.

"The second thing—and I can only hope you believe me—is that, other than the first night we met, I've never lied to you. Hedged a couple of times, maybe, like when you asked me if I knew any of those bastards and I avoided giving you an answer at all. I'm sure as hell not proud of what I've done, but I could never have forgiven myself or let Glenn go if I hadn't done it.

"Third and most important of all is that everything I told you the other night, about us, is true. I loved Glenn more than life itself, but Glenn is gone, and the last thing I could do for him I've done. You're here, now, and I've only begun to realize how important you've become to me. Please believe that. Please."

I believed it.

"And I wouldn't be sitting here, spilling my guts out to you, if I didn't think you feel pretty much the same way about me. We aren't two starry-eyed kids; we're two adult men who just happen to be gay and who, I think, can grow to need and love one another."

Ed brought his palms off the dresser and folded his hands, loosely, between his legs, his wrists on his thighs. "The defense rests," he said.

I found myself putting on the socks I was taking from the dresser when I'd found Glenn's photo. Ed was right, of course. I did care for him, more than I could ever remember caring for anyone before.

I reached for my pants and slipped them on. But Ed had killed eight men! Regardless of what complete shits they may have been, did they deserve to die for what they'd done? What about their friends and lovers...didn't they hurt, too?

Standing up, I walked to the open closet and took a shirt off a hanger. It was very improbable that the police would ever solve the case. The deaths had stopped; there wouldn't be any more—I believed Ed on that score. The debt had been paid. The police, increasingly relieved as time wore on with no new cyanide deaths, could put the entire string of deaths into the "Unsolved" file and get on to other things.

Why had I never thought of Ed as a suspect? That part was easy; like Martin Bell and Gary Miller and everyone else including the police who never questioned the deaths too closely, I believed what I wanted to believe. And I wanted to believe Ed was not involved.

Buttoning the last button of my shirt, I realized I had one button left over. Looking down, I saw the bottom of the shirt was uneven. Sighing, I unbuttoned from top to bottom and started all over again. What good would it do to turn Ed in—or having him turn himself in? Would it bring any one of the eight men back? If I were Ed, wouldn't I have done exactly what he did? I suspected very strongly that I just might.

Tucking in my shirttail, I zipped up my fly and reached under the bed for my shoes. But could I let somebody who had caused eight deaths go scot-free? Just because I might love him?

Sitting back down on the edge of the bed, I put my shoes on, wiping a smudge off one toe with my thumb. I'd been a loner most of my life. I could be a loner again, and I'd survive. Sure, and I could be Robinson Crusoe if I had to be, or a monk. But did I want to? I had a pretty good idea of what life could be like with Ed, if I'd let it be. The question was, did I want it? Did I want it bad enough?

Getting up from the bed, I walked toward the door. Ed was still sitting on the dresser, watching me.

"I've got to think for a minute," I said, opening the door. "We'll talk when I get back, okay?"

Ed nodded. "Okay," he said.

I closed the door behind me, and leaned my back against it. I was dizzy and my legs felt like they were going to give out. What in hell was I going to do? Go against everything I've prided myself on all my life: my sense of doing what had to be done just because it was right? Or spend the rest of my life going to bed alone with my principles, dreaming about someone and something I'd let slip away? What the hell should I do?

But I didn't have to ask, really. I knew the answer.

Pushing myself away from the door with my shoulders, I walked down the hallway toward the elevator.

YOUR PRIMARY SOURCE

for print books and e-books

Gay, Lesbian, Bisexual

on the Internet at

http://www.glbpubs.com

e-Book Fiction by such leading authors as:

Bill Lee
Mike Newman
Byrd Roberts
Mike Newman
Gene-Michael Higney
Robert Peters
Marsh Cassady

Glenn Hough
Chris Kent
William Tarvin
Veronica Cas
Kurt Kendall
Jim Brogan
Richard Dann

and of course, Dorien Grey

**Works available for downloads
(as low as $1 per short story)
in a wide variety of formats to
suit your particular taste and style**